An

ODDITY

of

SOME

CONSEQUENCE

D1369656

An

ODDITY

of

SOME

CONSEQUENCE

GARY DICKSON

Pairings, Ltd.

Published by Pairings, Ltd., Los Angeles, California
www.garydickson.us

GIRL FRIDAY
PRODUCTIONS·

Edited and designed by Girl Friday Productions
www.girlfridayproductions.com

Cover design: Danielle Christopher
Project management: Bethany Davis

Image credits: Cover © Shutterstock/Mayer George

ISBN (paperback): 978-1-7344015-0-9
ISBN (ebook): 978-1-7344015-1-6
Library of Congress Control Number: 2019920887

First edition

To my wife, Susie
Nothing odd, all consequential

That willing suspension of disbelief for the moment,
which constitutes poetic faith.

—Samuel Taylor Coleridge

ONE

Martin, the leader of the coffee klatch regulars, insisted that Robert, the newcomer, had to be younger than the forty-eight he claimed. But Robert had looked the same since forever—well, at least since 1789, at the beginning of the French Revolution. From then on, he never seemed to age. When he had asked his mother why he wasn't beginning to show any of those telltale but fine wrinkles at the corners of his eyes that he'd noticed in others his age, she had said without a blink of an eye that it must have been that tonic she had given him when he was a child, an elixir from an old recipe handed down from her great-aunt. It was an herbal blend of an exotic origin, and she seemed to remember that it was generously enriched with spices from the Orient, heavy on ginseng, she said with a wry smile.

But by the time it was apparent that he wasn't going to age, his mother was gone, and if there were any truth to be known, it too was gone with her. Did the concoction have anything to do with his longevity? There were no answers, and Robert had stopped looking for an explanation many years before, because there was none. Modern medicine and the science of DNA were another hundred years away.

***

At six feet, one inch, or 185 centimeters, Robert was over half a foot taller than the average man in eighteenth-century France, where and when he was born. And at forty-eight, he was an old man by the standard of those times, having already outlived the normal lifespan by ten years. Nevertheless, he had survived a remarkable nine generations and remained in perfect health—and he still had all his hair, and no wrinkles to speak of. And while he had lived through several wars, he had never been wounded or been in any accident that had resulted in more than a cut or scrape. The illnesses of childhood, like measles and chickenpox, had affected him in much the same way as they had affected other children—except he endured while some didn't. He was uncertain as to how he could or would die.

During his first hundred or so years, he was, at times, preoccupied looking for signs of aging. When would his real age begin to show? But he never saw any degeneration due to age. He was not only strong, but some also said he was handsome. His hair was light brown, his eyes blue, and his complexion fair but slightly ruddy. And whatever questions he had regarding the miracle of his appearance, he had learned to keep those to himself—and who was there to ask anyway?

Robert had moved from Rome to Beverly Hills, and Martin and his buddies of the little club on Santa Monica were only the latest doubters in a long line. They seemed reluctant to let him join their group that met every morning at the Café Malmaison in Beverly Hills. On his first day, and for several mornings thereafter, he had sat by himself at a nearby table, careful not to encroach on their space, which, although unreserved, was nonetheless respected by everyone. After he had been there every day for more than two weeks as routinely as they were, they relented and motioned for him to join them. No words were exchanged just yet, only a subtle hand signal, but it was a welcome gesture from Robert's perspective.

The introductions and perfunctory questions had dribbled out over the next few days. And the only comment on Robert's answers came from Martin Marans, the designated elder of the Malmaison senior society—the others always followed his lead. "So, if you're from Rome, you must be Italian?"

"I lived in Rome, but I'm French," Robert said.

Robert waited, but there was no follow-up. That was a relief. It was a long story, a very long story. But he knew Martin was mulling over his response. Slightly balding but in good shape otherwise, probably in his mid- to late sixties, his face revealed contemplation mixed with a dose of doubt. There would be a follow-up, and when it came, it would be a carefully thought-out one.

Robert could see on Martin's face and the faces of some of the others that the absence of a more elaborate response as to who he was and what he was doing there was a little unsettling. They had questions, but for the moment they restrained themselves from asking more. They wanted to be nosy without appearing so. Robert had noticed that, in general, people liked to be able to check off a few boxes of similarity to themselves to be comfortable.

The Malmaison was known for its strong coffee, its Viennese pastries, in opposition to its name, and its liberal policy of letting customers linger. The café hadn't been hard to identify as a hangout, and the bonus for Robert was that he lived nearby. Near enough that he could walk there, if the weather was good, which it always was. Even when it did rain, it was brief. The weather was agreeable even in winter.

The place was furnished with uncomfortable French café chairs with skeleton backs and red faux-leather seats that encircled equally Spartan wooden tables with tiled tops. Smarter places constructed of chrome and glass, like the ones where young professionals gathered before work, stood on every corner in Beverly Hills, so the Malmaison was unique in that regard. The only category of business whose number exceeded the coffee emporiums in L.A. was the hairdresser. But Café Malmaison was the place for a particular demographic, one where Robert fit in better than some others.

It opened more or less promptly at 6:45—early by L.A. standards. Cars—expensive cars, not the high-performance variety that the young favored, but luxury sedans, plush and comfortable for older tuchuses—crowded the metered parking spaces in front of the café even a few minutes before it opened. These were the habitués, mature men retired after working thirty, forty years or more, accustomed to a lifetime of getting up before dawn. Retirement didn't change their clocks. Plus, their wives, if they still had them, were glad for the time alone.

This fraternity of retirees, cronies to the core, were all in their early sixties to late seventies. And while their clique professed to be open to select contemporaries, unwritten conditions applied. It was unclear what these conditions might be, although Robert was sure that a certain maturity was a prerequisite. Robert admitted to forty-eight, a whippersnapper by their standards, but he could have chosen almost any age. Some, including Martin, likely thought he had lied about his age in order to qualify for the group. They left little doubt that he was, at best, a junior associate, not a partner yet.

And while he appeared to be young, even younger than he said he was, he knew that he had experience going for him. Over the last 270-plus years, it had not been difficult to understand that prudence dictated that he guard the secret of his age. Besides, he had lost track of his exact age. He did know that he was born around 1741 in Paris, although his family's roots were in a small town near Orléans about eighty miles southwest of the capital.

Blessed with a better-than-average memory, Robert Valmer knew firsthand that which others knew only from books. But while history for him was experience, it wasn't as if he had a firm grip on the entirety of the epic he had lived. Lapses were inevitable, and there were certain periods of time when he couldn't recall exactly what had transpired. He didn't have shades of amnesia; no, it was more as if the quantity of years he had lived had exceeded his ability to remember them in detail. As a result, only the most consequential episodes of his life stood out clearly from the haze. Those could be summoned to conscious description rather easily. Still, there was a lot to remember.

He had to be careful, as just one careless remark could open Pandora's box. There would be questions. Questions he couldn't or shouldn't answer. But given who he was, he wasn't devoid of ego. It happened sometimes after too much wine. On such occasions, he might brag about some fact from a previous era that only an eyewitness could provide. Most of the time, people dismissed these blurted revelations as exaggerations or jokes. And he was always relieved and would laugh along, promising himself never to open his mouth like that again. Yet promises were easier made than kept.

Keeping his own counsel for two hundred years had produced its own challenges. Being guarded about his past was a habit that, when followed consistently, resulted in very few relationships. Even his marriages had suffered from a lack of intimacy due to his secrecy.

Just two years prior, he had been enjoying a sublime life in Italy with his third wife, Arianna. Then the unspeakable had happened. In the prime of her life, after they had been married only a few years, she was struck with terminal, virulent cancer. A few months after the diagnosis, she died, and Robert found himself burying his young wife in a solemn ceremony in a prominent plot of the Campo Verano cemetery in Rome. In the middle of winter, in the middle of the day, Robert was the only mourner, not counting the officiating priest. Her parents had died since their marriage, and in any case, the family had disowned Arianna when she insisted on marrying Robert over their objections, especially her brother's. No friends attended either, since Robert and Arianna had always preferred their own company, excluding others from their circle.

Even the weather had conspired to accentuate the bleakness of the event. A slow drizzle fell, soaking the scene while a damp cold settled in, numbing Robert's feet and hands. He listened and waited for the priest's prayers and supplications to God to admit the soul of his beloved Arianna. His mind went numb as well.

Finally, it was over, and then he wasn't thinking of the funeral but of the previous six months since the diagnosis of terminal ovarian cancer. Arianna's acceptance of the verdict had been more resigned than his. He'd convinced himself that something could be done. He had pleaded with her to seek out the most advanced and exotic therapies and medicines, but she was deeply religious and had instead spent her time preparing for the inevitable. God's will, as she put it.

She was braver than he. He felt cheated. He hated the God that he didn't believe in.

His mourning of Arianna had lasted for more months than convention required while he tried to find the courage to begin yet again. He had tinkered with the idea of returning to Paris, but the memories waiting there were more painful even than those lurking in Rome. Robert had started over more than once—many times, in fact. But where would it be this time? It needed to be somewhere completely new. He had never tried the United States. What was less like Europe than Los Angeles? And that's how he decided.

In the past, whenever he knew that it was time to move on, it was always deeply disturbing to him as well as to any relationships he had established. How was he to explain the fact that everyone around him kept aging while he remained the same? There had been those occasions when the difference had become so apparent that it had been necessary to sever his ties just to avoid the mounting visual evidence of his unique status. Keeping a low profile was paramount. To this end, he maintained homes in several different countries, traveling quite often, and he was never in the same place for long periods of time. He and his first wife had divorced when their three children were very young. She had promptly moved to Vienna and taken the children with her. It was a bitter split, and over time Robert had been forced to abandon his role as their father. That was so long ago now that it no longer impacted him emotionally, but it taught him to steel himself against developing any history or any notoriety that would draw attention to himself or would necessitate that he should provide documents someone might trace.

The one constant was his name. That he wouldn't give up, regardless of the risk, although the *de* had been dropped. And when he moved to Los Angeles, he swore that this time he would stay a loner; fewer explanations would demand less subterfuge.

Then one day he almost slipped up at Café Malmaison when he was tempted to recount a personal experience of long ago as his newfound friends argued a point. Each morning except Saturday and Sunday, the same men—no fewer than seven, and often as many as twelve—gathered to reminisce, bitch, compare, and compete, using their stories as leverage for their one-upmanship games. Newspapers were as much a part of their early morning as the coffee and croissants, providing topics like politics, business, or sports that they could argue or discuss. The *New York Post*, the *New York Times*, and the *Wall Street Journal* seemed to jump-start their conversations, as if a catalyst were needed. Their stories bridged the span of a couple of generations. They remembered a lot, but Robert Valmer, the new kid to the klatch, and to Beverly Hills, had a distinct advantage.

Don't be a show-off, he reminded himself.

The conversation had turned toward the oft-visited subjects of the failures of the wars in Iraq and Afghanistan. Alfred, second in command of the group after Martin, said, "Well, as long as we're discussing it, I can tell you that there's nothing that can compare to what I witnessed during the Tet Offensive." He was one of several Vietnam vets in the group.

"You're right, Alfred. War is war, but in Vietnam we got mixed up in a civil war. They're the bloodiest of all. Look at our own Civil War, for God's sake," E. W. said, putting his two cents in. E. W. was short for Edward William.

"Well, E. W., I wasn't around for the Civil War, like you," Alfred said, laughing.

Robert could have told them a thing or two about civil wars and revolutions, where brother was pitted against brother, friend against friend, and often to the death. Just the word "revolution" evoked the most vivid recollections of Paris in 1789. Should he tell them about the barricades, he wondered, the street fighting, and his cousin, Philippe, bleeding red after being hit in the head by a cobblestone near the Palais-Royal?

He and Philippe had traveled to Paris from the Château de Valmer in the Loire Valley near Orléans to rescue their aunt, his father's sister-in-law. Entering the city through the Porte de Choisy on the left bank of the Seine, they had been forced to abandon their horses and don the most ordinary clothes: leather pants with drawstrings, loose-fitting blouses of flax and leather, and laborer hats with wide brims that concealed their faces. Royals weren't welcome in Paris, and that was the reason they had come. Their uncle, Count Guillaume de Valmer, was already confined in the Bastille. Now their aunt was alone except for a few servants, who could turn on her from one moment to the next. Robert and Philippe had to help her escape to the south.

To reach the Valmer apartments in the Place des Vosges in the fourth arrondissement meant making their way across the Seine using the Pont Neuf bridge. And it was just after they had crossed and were proceeding down the rue Royale that they came across a gang of ruffians, thankfully not armed with firearms but with truncheons, bottles, and stones. Philippe and Robert couldn't afford confronting them outnumbered and unarmed, so they darted into a side street, but not before they had been spotted and then chased. The raised voices and shouts and the general hullabaloo told them that the gang chasing them down the street was gaining on them, as the sounds of footfalls on the cobblestones grew louder. Running as fast as he could, Robert grabbed Philippe's arm to pull him down another side street. It was at that moment that Philippe was struck in the head by a cobblestone.

"Robert, you seem to be far away. Don't you have something to add?" Martin had asked, interrupting his remembrances.

"Alfred and E. W. have it right. Whether war or revolution, violence is grotesque," Robert said.

"Robert, you must have been part of the diplomatic corps," E. W. said.

"Not even close," Robert said.

"So, what *did* you do in Italy?" Alfred asked.

Robert had wondered when that was coming. And he had argued with himself about what he should tell them when it did. He couldn't tell them anything about positions he had held that they might investigate, and they no doubt would.

"I managed investments."

"What kind of investments?" E. W. asked.

"Currencies."

"Sounds risky," Martin said.

"Quite so, the risk having everything to do with the reward."

The morning meeting ended on that note, and as they were leaving the Café Malmaison in twos and threes, Martin asked Robert if he could give him a lift.

"Thank you, but I don't live far," Robert said.

"Oh, come on, let me drop you off," Martin said.

Martin's Bentley, a two-door coupé convertible, was directly in front of the café, the director's spot. Robert crawled in.

"OK, where to?" Martin said.

"I live on Rodeo, just above Carmelita," Robert said.

"We're almost neighbors. I envy that you can walk to the café every morning. We live on North Crescent above Sunset, near the Beverly Hills Hotel. Do you know it?"

"I know the hotel."

In less than five minutes, Martin stopped in front of Robert's house. It was a two-story English Tudor of some size. Robert had purchased the house and the adjoining lot sight unseen—if photographs on the Internet were discounted—while he was still living in Rome. He was a man who knew what he wanted. When he arrived in Beverly Hills, he had employed one of L.A.'s leading interior designers, commissioning her to completely renovate and furnish the house. And while the construction went on and on, he lived in a hotel nearby, supervising the progress.

An award-winning landscaping firm had handled reworking the extensive grounds in the front of the home as well as on the sides and back areas, where the pool and tennis court were. The climates of L.A. and Rome are not dissimilar, so many of the plantings including the palms, oleander, and bougainvillea were familiar in a reassuring way. Compared to the worn-out condition of the house when he had started the renovation, it was now a mansion.

"My wife, Mimi, and I saw the house being redone. We passed it almost daily going into Beverly Hills and wondered who in the hell had so much money." Martin laughed.

"It got a little out of hand."

"Doesn't it always? By the way, if you're not busy, maybe you can go out with us to dinner on Friday night, just another couple, old friends, and my daughter. What do you think? We'll have a drink at our house first around seven."

"Sure, that would be nice. Thank you," Robert said.

TWO

Robert arrived at seven minutes after seven. It wasn't polite to be precisely on time, yet not rudely late. There were two cars already there, one Mercedes and another Bentley, not Martin's, at the end of the long drive in front of the house, a low-slung, rambling California ranch landscaped with large palms and willows and well-tended beds of flowers and shrubs.

He was going to ring the bell, but before he could press the button, Martin opened the door and greeted him. Taking him by the arm, chatting all the while, he led Robert through the foyer, through the great room, and onto a patio that extended from the house to the pool. Robert saw the other guests standing near an outdoor bar.

"Hey, guys, this is Robert. Robert Valmer, my new French friend. Robert, this is my wife, Mimi; George and Erica Carlson, our oldest friends; and my daughter, Alexis."

Robert knew that when you're the new member of a group, a disproportionate amount of attention is focused on either verifying or disproving what has been previously reported about you. Mimi exhibited the posture of a self-assured and confident woman. Behind those eyes of green Robert saw intelligence and experience. He understood where the power lay in this family.

The Carlsons were about the same age as the Marans. George was fair and blue-eyed, reinforcing the likely Scandinavian origin of his name. His wife, Erica, was blonde, very pretty, trim, with a generous smile. They looked a perfect couple. She obviously followed fashion, as her outfit revealed her interest: wide palazzo pants, an animal-print silk blouse with an embellishing necklace, and chunky rings.

And then there was Alexis, the daughter, obviously the star of the show. Robert all at once felt a little dumb, because now he realized that Martin perceived himself as a matchmaker. The Carlsons and the Marans were there for decoration only. Alexis was the main event. But from what Robert could see, Alexis wouldn't need the services of her father. She appeared to be quite capable of attracting whomever she might want.

She was beautiful with dark eyes and jet-black hair, tall and thin but undeniably female, and Robert saw in her eyes the same depth of awareness and understanding that he saw in her mother's. He wouldn't guess at her age—that would be impolite—but she was undoubtedly younger than even his claimed age. She was dressed in the Beverly Hills uniform of form-fitting black skinny pants and a luxurious top of silk, lace, and shiny stones. A large belt with a jewel-encrusted buckle advertised her slight waist.

This was exactly the kind of situation that Robert had promised himself he would avoid. Relationships with women had a way of developing far beyond what he had experienced as prudent. But maybe he was making too much of it all. Maybe he had been invited as a gesture of friendship rather than as a potential suitor of Martin's daughter. After all, coincidences do happen.

"Don't you find that coffee klatch a little boring?" Mimi asked. "Every morning, always the same thing."

"Not at all," Robert said. "I enjoy the conversation."

"I can see my father must have given you some instruction," Alexis said.

"He didn't, but what should he have told me?" Robert said.

"That remains to be seen."

"Mr. Valmer," said Erica, "Martin tells us you lived in Rome. It's such a beautiful city. Where did you live?"

"Near the Pantheon."

"I know exactly where that is," Erica said.

"And why did you leave Italy, Mr. Valmer?" George asked.

"I wanted to live in the United States. Please, call me Robert."

"But why Los Angeles?" asked Alexis.

"The weather."

After a flute of champagne, Martin organized the descent into Beverly Hills, where they would have dinner. Martin instructed that the Carlsons would drive their car, Martin and Mimi would take theirs, and Alexis would ride with Robert to show him the way. Robert smiled inwardly. Martin thought himself clever. Their destination was less than fifteen minutes away.

"You must forgive Martin," Alexis said.

"There's nothing to forgive. Does he do this often?" He had been right. It wasn't a coincidence.

"Yes, quite."

"He must not be very good at it."

"Why do you say that?"

"Because he's still doing it," he said. "You must be picky."

"There's little doubt."

"By the way, is it an American custom to call your father by his first name rather than 'Father' or 'Dad'?"

"It's a Marans custom. When I got my graduate degree, he said for equality's sake I should address him as Martin. So, I obliged."

"He's very generous."

"But I still call him Father when I'm mad."

***

They arrived at the restaurant, e. baldi, and sat at a corner table. It was a small, intimate bistro where everyone fit tightly together. Accented with soft lighting, plaintive Italian music in the background spelled intimacy and romance. Martin's seating instructions had Robert and Alexis sitting side by side.

Robert perused the menu. From the look of it, he could have been in Italy. All the waiters were Italian. He recognized several accents: Florentine, Umbrian, and even Roman. When it was his turn, he asked a few questions and then ordered in Italian. The waiters seemed pleased.

"Your Italian is apparently very good, based on the waiters' response," Alexis said. "How long did you live in Rome?"

"Most recently for a few years, but I had lived there before, too."

"Martin said that you were into currency trading."

"I dabble."

"That's considered highly speculative, isn't it?"

"It can be."

"By the way, do you realize that you haven't asked me one question?"

"I haven't?"

"Why not?" she asked. "Not interested?"

"I wouldn't say that. I'm sure if you want me to know something, then you'll tell me."

"Most people aren't that patient."

"In French we have a saying that patience is the mother of virtue."

"I agree that it has its rewards, but I'm afraid we live in a time when immediacy, the cult of *now*, is king."

"I'm not unfamiliar with the motivation, just uncertain of its benefits."

"My dear Robert, you are not only an arbitrager but a philosopher as well."

"I can confide in you that I know a lot more about euros and yuans than I do about Plato and Aristotle."

"Somehow I'm not convinced. I think you know a lot more than you're prepared to reveal."

"I'm pacing myself."

"It seems you two have struck up a friendship," Martin said. "Remember us?"

"I apologize for being rude. It was my fault for asking Alexis so many questions," Robert said. From her chuckle it appeared that Alexis appreciated his humor.

Martin winked when he said, "I'm only kidding. I'm glad we've had a good time."

That remark signaled that dinner was over, and while they were standing on the sidewalk waiting for the valet to bring the cars around, Alexis said, "You know, it's silly for you to drive me back to my parents' house. I can just ride with them."

"You're not going to get away that easily, unless it's your preference," Robert said. They were both fishing.

She smiled with a knowing look and said, "Well, if you insist."

"And I absolutely do." He was certain that was the right answer. She seemed pleased; not a woman easily dismissed. When they arrived back at the Marans', Martin and Mimi were already inside, leaving Robert and Alexis to themselves.

"We could do this again sometime if you like, without chaperones," Alexis said. She was a modern woman. He liked that.

***

On Monday, Robert arrived early at Café Malmaison. Martin was seated at his usual spot at the head of the table; the others hadn't arrived yet. Robert was glad because it gave him the chance to thank Martin for inviting him to dinner and to express how much he had enjoyed meeting his wife, the Carlsons, and Alexis.

"I think Alexis might like you," Martin said.

"Did she say so?" Robert asked.

"No, but she didn't scold me for inviting her to meet a total loser, as she terms most of the men that I've introduced her to in the past."

"I can't imagine she needs your help."

"She doesn't think so either."

"Anything else?"

"She said you didn't ask her anything about herself. Is there anything you'd like to know?"

"I'm quite certain that she'll tell me what she wants me to know."

Robert could see a look of disappointment spread over Martin's face. His eyes drooped; his smile retracted. He had wanted to give Robert the sales pitch on Alexis. And Robert was struggling, urging himself to go slow in spite of how intrigued he was by Alexis. But the last thing he needed was someone asking him a lot of questions—she seemed the type—or worse, researching him on the Internet, if she hadn't already.

Based on her complaint, it would seem that the best strategy to avoid being questioned would be to ask a lot of them himself, but he had learned long ago that if you asked questions, then reciprocity obligated you to answer whatever is asked. She probably knew this as well. This course of action didn't always lead to happy results.

He had been in Los Angeles for just over a year and had been strict about limiting his contact with anyone, particularly women. Women meant intimacy; they thrive on it, and are unhappy when deprived of it. During the renovation of his house, it had been easier to stay busy, but now that it was complete, he was a little lonely and a lot bored. The company of men had never been enough for Robert. Martin had been right. Alexis was a catch: irresistibly beautiful, obviously intelligent, a woman in every way. But therein lay the danger; the very qualities that so attracted him could be the same ones that could unmask him.

Martin didn't give up. He slid a card over with a telephone number, winked, and said, "Just in case."

"Look, I'm going to call her. Did anyone ever tell you that you worry too much?"

"Everyone. It's what I'm known for."

"I understand why."

***

Just in case came two days later. Robert knew that the etiquette of introductions dictated that he not let the week expire without touching base with Alexis. The number rang once, twice, and on the fifth ring an answering device picked up and said, "You have reached the offices of Dr. Alexis Roth. She is in session now. Please leave your name and a brief message." He left his name and number.

In session? Dr. Roth? What did that mean? Maybe he *should* have asked a few questions when he had the chance. Who used the term "in session"? A psychiatrist, perhaps.

An hour later she returned his call. "Sorry I missed your call."

"No problem," Robert said. "I was wondering if you'd like to have lunch on Saturday. I thought we might drive up the Pacific Coast Highway. I've been told there's a nice restaurant near Pepperdine University."

"I'd love to. I guess you're talking about Geoffrey's. It's lovely."

"Right, Geoffrey's. Let's say I pick you up around noon? It'll take about an hour on Saturday with the beach traffic."

She gave him her address and explained that it was a high-rise condominium tower on Avenue of the Stars in Century City; it was only ten minutes from his home. He recognized the building from the address and her description. It was the premier condominium residence in Beverly Hills.

He would have loved to ask her what she was in session about. There might be more questions than he'd originally thought.

THREE

Saturday came quickly enough, and when Robert arrived at Alexis's building, he was required to stop at the security post and give his name so that they could announce his arrival. The structure itself was an iconic tower with a sandstone façade rising forty-one stories in the shape of an ellipse. The building had been featured often in design circles, particularly in architectural and interior magazines. The tower occupied a footprint of several acres that included a tropical garden, an Olympic pool, a spa and exercise facility, and all the other luxuries one might think of or expect. When he arrived, a team of valets took his car, and he entered the imposing lobby, sat in front of the fireplace, and waited.

It wasn't long before he saw Alexis walking from the elevators toward him. She was dressed in a casual, chic outfit of white cotton pants, a soft gold sweater, and a lemon-yellow leather bomber jacket. Her shoes, somewhere between sensible and scary, were four-inch-high, open-toed sandals of a caramel color matching her handbag. She wore just the right amount of gold jewelry. He gave her the French air kiss on both cheeks, feeling he might need to live up to any French myth she might have.

Seeing that she wore her hair swept back in a ponytail, he asked, "Would you like me to put the top down?"

"Why not? We are in L.A., you know. It's a lovely drive along the coast through Malibu and then up to Pepperdine."

On the way, the conversation was of the warm-up variety, nothing too serious, just the weather, the news, but no politics and no religion. She was clearly practical. He liked that.

Geoffrey's was built on the cliff side of the Pacific Coast Highway above the blue waters of the ocean. Malibu was visible toward the south, and the restaurant seemed to hang suspended over the beach. A patio interrupted by native plantings of grasses and cacti, bottle palms, and ficus shrubs offered many out-of-the-way nooks for guests seeking privacy. It was romantic, even in daylight, but at night it had to be glorious, Robert thought. They were escorted to a table at the railing overlooking the water. They both ordered the lobster salad, and Robert selected a good Sancerre. Alexis settled in and waited a moment before she said, "My father says that you're forty-eight. You look younger."

"Thank you. That's good, isn't it?" *Uh oh*, he thought. *Here we go with the age questions.*

"I'm forty, but I say that I'm thirty-nine." She smiled coquettishly.

"A woman's prerogative."

"I was married, but my husband died. That was eight years ago."

Robert reasoned that she offered this to elicit a telling of his own history. "I'm sorry," he said.

"Once again, I seem to be providing all the questions as well as all the answers."

"And you're doing a fine job, too."

"I'm trying to figure out if you're coy or secretive." She said this with a tone that indicated a slight but definite annoyance.

"I can save you some time; I'm neither. I'm quiet."

"I don't think so. I think you're secretive." This was said more as a question than a statement. She wanted him to deny it, but more so, she wanted him to prove it by telling her everything.

"Not really. What do you want to know?"

"Have you ever been married?"

"Yes, twice. First wife divorced. We were too young. Second deceased, two years ago." A little license was necessary. She wasn't going to give up.

The lobster came at the right moment. The waiter intruding on her thoughts had perhaps broken her concentration. Might a little wine reduce the tension? He signaled the waiter to pour some more.

"Are you curious about what I do?" she asked.

"I wasn't, because I hadn't realized you worked. But when the voicemail said something about your being in session, I did wonder what kind of session."

"I'm a metaphysical psychologist."

"Ah. And in English?"

"In the vernacular, some might say that I'm a psychic: in French, a clairvoyant, at least that's what some of my patients like to think."

"And in reality?"

"I depend on my doctorate in psychology. And I supplement that with my experience and intuition. It's not clairvoyance, but patients believe what they need to believe to stumble onto the truth. Sometimes a little mystery facilitates understanding."

After that admission, or more accurately, revelation, Robert lapsed into silence, trying to find the right thing to say. If he were to express approval and admiration, she would probably think it flattery. And if he expressed any doubt, she might interpret that as ridicule and be offended. She made it easy for him.

"Not that many people need to know the future," she said.

"I would think everyone would."

"Most people are afraid to."

"If they have any appreciation of the past, I can understand their reluctance."

"You're not really looking for a relationship, are you?"

"I wasn't, but you rarely find one when you're looking."

"Do you like sex, Robert?"

"Is that a question you usually open with, or do you always ask that on the second date?"

"Are we dating? If so, then technically this is our first date."

"You are very precise."

"Precision avoids misunderstanding, and it's why I asked you if you like sex . . . more precisely, heterosexual sex?"

"Oh, now I understand. You must have had some forays with some men who perhaps were of a different persuasion."

"It's not uncommon here in L.A. And although charming, it can be . . . how can I be kind?"

"Without a future?"

"Exactly."

"I can assure you that I'm a man dedicated to the distaff category."

"Sounds more clinical than romantic."

"But precise. I might surprise you."

"You already have."

Had she had a reason to clear that up? What would happen when they got back to her condominium? Would she invite him up? Coy she was not. They took the long way back, deserting the coast road, taking one of the canyon trails and backtracking and winding their way through the Palisades until they fell on the 405. Exiting on Sunset, they were soon at her condo. It was close to five o'clock in the afternoon. He wondered if she was thinking what he was thinking. He would find out shortly.

Before getting out of the car, Alexis leaned over and gave him a kiss on the cheek and thanked him for a lovely afternoon and the interesting conversation. And before he could compose a fitting answer, she was out of the car but seemed to hesitate a moment, perhaps for the last word or maybe something from him.

Whenever a man invites a woman to his house, there is always the distinct possibility that he has more in mind than just showing her his stamp collection. He decided to see her response.

"Would you like to come over for a casual dinner at my place tomorrow evening?" Robert asked.

"No. But I would like to get to know you better. But you know what that means."

"No, what?"

"You'll have to tell me about yourself," she said.

"Why don't you just look into your crystal ball?"

"Because you can't see in if someone has the curtains drawn."

"So, when will I see you again?" Robert asked.

"Tomorrow, but I'll meet you in the Polo Lounge at the Beverly Hills Hotel at 6:30."

Alexis was going to be a challenge. Her alternative suggestion of the Polo Lounge was not spontaneous. She had held that in reserve for just the right moment. He had to be careful. Dr. Roth was clearly two steps ahead.

Sunday was a long day. He was waiting, even pacing, for 6:30. To pass time, he decided to google "Dr. Alexis Marans Roth," and when the search results appeared, she dominated the first two pages. There was a LinkedIn page, a Facebook page, some *New York Times* articles, Alexis's own site, and other entries pertaining to her professional and social life. He wouldn't need to ask many questions. It was all here.

Alexis was indeed forty, born in L.A., had graduated from UCLA undergrad and Stanford with a doctorate in psychology. He learned from an article in the *Hollywood Reporter* that she owned a company, Alexis, Inc., where she "interprets the dreams, reveals the future, and coaches the success" of her clients. A number of glowing reviews by Hollywood stars testified as to her remarkable powers.

And he read about her deceased husband, Evan Roth of New York, an investment banker and art collector. From photographs contained in the articles, Robert learned that Mr. Roth had been twenty-five years senior to his wife and had died after a brief illness. It seemed from the various reports that he and Alexis had struggled with a bicoastal marriage—he was living in New York while she lived in L.A. They had been married five years when he died. Apparently the two had met at a summer party in the Hamptons, and if Robert could hazard a guess, they married ignoring the distance between the coasts and hoping that wedlock would overcome all obstacles. Hopeless optimism. She was smarter than that.

Digging deeper, he followed some of the citations leading to other websites, where he found that she had written several books on paranormal and metaphysical subjects. She was a guest professor at the Esalen Institute so regularly that she had been made a part of the permanent faculty, where she taught self-help courses. Apparently, she worked from a suite of offices located in a building in Beverly Hills—the AMR building on Canon near Wilshire. AMR, Alexis Marans Roth, it couldn't be a coincidence. She had plenty of business savvy as well.

After an hour, he stopped reading, although he could have gone on and on. Alexis was so accomplished that she was intimidating. She had a thriving business, was a respected authority on psychology and metaphysics, and was beautiful too. Robert wondered why she was interested in him . . . if she even was. Maybe she would tell him tonight.

Robert decided to google himself. He knew she would, so he might as well know what she might read. Only two entries surfaced, each more or less the same: "Robert Valmer, French, Paris, Rome, Los Angeles, investments." He had always lived a low-profile life, moving around Europe without establishing any traceable roots. His lack of biography had the potential of eliciting more scrutiny than he might like. And he told himself that Alexis was exactly the kind of person he should avoid: intelligent, sophisticated, and curious.

He had to recognize that his previous relationships with women throughout his life, his wives and his lovers, had been with European women. Arianna, his deceased wife, was Italian, and traditional. These modern American women were of a different cut altogether, and Alexis was a prime example: accomplished, proficient, and most of all, independent. And that is where the danger lay. In a relationship where there is an equality of partners in almost every domain, there is also the expectation of transparency. And that was the exact quality that Robert could least afford, and the one most in demand by Alexis. He had been through this before.

Twenty-five years before meeting Arianna, he had found it necessary to leave Geneva to terminate a maturing relationship with a beautiful and talented Swiss woman, Jacqueline, from a prominent family. Their courtship had lasted a year, and they were destined to be married. Everyone in Geneva society approved, but Robert had failed to recognize the inquisitiveness of Jacqueline's mother. And it wasn't what she had found out about Robert; rather, it was disturbing to her that there seemed to be nothing to find. His current status was easily uncovered: rich, respected, intelligent, and well positioned. But what of his past? Where had he come from? Where had the *money* come from?

Before it could escalate into a cause célèbre, he knew that the only course was to give Jacqueline up in order to avoid a more thorough inquisition. He broke her heart. He broke his own as well. But how could he have shared his past without revealing his most well-kept secret? He knew that his actions made him seem heartless, and for that reason over the next twenty-five years, he managed to avoid any liaisons with women that might morph into something more substantial than a fling until he met Arianna. It wasn't what he wanted. He was just like everyone else. He longed for love and companionship, but the question was, at what price? And now fate had presented this charming person in the form of Alexis. Her delicate gestures and subtle movements were as beautiful as her mind. She was so very desirable that he hoped he wouldn't regret breaking his rule of not getting involved. But there was still the chance that she might not be interested other than for his novelty. That might be a good outcome.

Robert arrived at the rendezvous point early since the Beverly Hills Hotel was only two blocks from his home. He passed through the lobby to the Polo Lounge, indicating to the maître d' that he was expected by Dr. Roth. She hadn't arrived yet, he was informed, but would he like to be seated at her table? He agreed and was shown to one of the two roomy booths with a command of the bar, the restaurant, and the door.

Robert knew the reputation of the Polo Lounge. So many movie stars had stayed and even lived at the hotel and frequented the bar and the pool that there was a cavalcade of photos displayed documenting the history of Hollywood. The décor of soft greens, natural woods, and the indoor-outdoor feel of the space engendered the coziness of a club. Robert easily imagined how many negotiations, both economic and romantic, must have been arranged on these premises. It seemed more like a movie set than a commercial establishment.

Seated where he was, he saw Alexis coming through the lobby. She stopped for a man in a dark suit who intercepted her; he shook her offered hand, and they exchanged a few words. During their brief conversation, she spied Robert and gave a little sign of recognition. Robert guessed that the man was one of the officials of the hotel. Alexis patiently stood there chatting, shifting her weight from one high heel to the other, her black dress with white polka dots clinging to her figure.

"I'm late," she said, sliding in beside him in the booth.

"No, I'm early. Would you like a glass of champagne?" Robert asked.

"No, *Robert*," she said, pronouncing his name in the French manner where the "t" is silent. "When at the Polo Lounge, we drink martinis, gin martinis with olives. I like the ones stuffed with anchovy. By the way, this was the favorite booth of Marilyn Monroe."

The waiter came over, and Robert, or rather *Robert*, ordered two gin martinis with Gibson gin and the preferred olive. He thought he could detect that she was impressed. Gibson was an old-timey gin and the gold standard for martini lovers. He was fortunate that she knew that piece of trivia. Little things like his knowledge of things past were at times out of sync with his purported age of forty-eight.

"I don't often admit it, but I googled you," she said.

"I didn't think you needed Google," he teased.

"I sometimes need to resort to other powers. Google didn't have much."

"I'm low-key."

"If you were any lower key, you wouldn't exist. How do you manage it?"

"I don't do anything notable. I've always been very private, never worked for any company, and I've always managed my own investments without outside assistance."

Her eyes had a quizzical look, indicating that his explanation had not quelled her curiosity, only whetted it. The martinis arrived, big ones, in a classic pedestal glass with two olives each, skewered by a bamboo toothpick dangling in the clear liquid. They picked up their glasses and clinked in a toast, their first.

"Here's to low-key," she said.

"Low-key and ESP," he teased.

"Are you making fun of what I do?"

He could tell that this wasn't a serious question but rather an attempt to receive affirmation. "I'm not *making* fun. I'm *having* fun."

"I would like your jokes better if they didn't seem to be at my expense." With this complaint, she produced a little pout of disapproval.

"I don't tease people I don't like."

"So, where did you go to school?" she asked, quickly shifting their conversation.

"The Sorbonne."

"And what did you study?" She looked at him expectantly. He knew he needed to give her a little.

"At first I studied economics, then later I studied archaeology."

"Why didn't you just pick subjects at opposite ends of the spectrum?"

"They're not that far apart. There's a lot of treasure to be dug up in archaeology." He couldn't help but laugh at his own joke, but instead of laughing, Alexis just stared at him.

"You're full of it, aren't you?"

"Do I need to be more serious?" he said, his smile faltering. "OK, I considered it, but I thought there was enough separation between the two to be interesting."

There was a pause. He guessed that the pace of the conversation was not to her liking. It was like a tennis match where all the points played are abbreviated, no long rallies of learning your opponent's strengths and more important, weaknesses. Then she began again.

"I had a similar experience, although my fields aren't quite as disparate as yours."

"Differences promote perspective."

"I'll write that down." She paused as if waiting. "Don't you want to ask me what I studied?"

"Sure, what?"

"Did anyone ever mention that you're difficult to talk to?"

"Perhaps it's my English." He smiled, knowing in advance that she would dismiss this excuse.

"No, your English is perfect. Where did you learn it?"

"Around."

"Around where?"

"Around the university, in Paris, books, newspapers, friends, everywhere."

"I studied French, but it's a difficult language. I've tried many times."

"The best way to learn French is to have a French lover."

"Sounds reasonable, sounds French. Have any ideas where I might find one?"

"We say in French, *tout est possible*, everything's possible."

They had already consumed two martinis each. Granted, it was at a leisurely pace, but the waiter didn't seem impatient. Robert assumed that Alexis graced the Polo Lounge frequently. He took her cue when she picked up the menu and began to scan the list of specialties. She decided on an omelet with fines herbes, and he opted for fettuccine Alfredo.

"It won't be as good as in Rome," Alexis said, opening both palms like the Italians do when frustrated.

"It's not on the menu often, so why not take a chance?"

"I could make it for you sometime. Mine's good."

"And you cook, too," he said.

"I love cooking." Alexis beamed as she said this.

"I do, too."

"I knew we would find something in common," she said, smiling.

Robert liked women with a sense of humor, and Alexis was quick and not at all stuffy. She had a directness with which he had little experience, but he was charmed that she risked offense to tease. And he noticed that silence didn't make her fidget. When the conversation paused, she wasn't in a hurry to find something or just anything to say.

They both used these intermezzos to delve into each other's eyes to check on what the other was thinking.

As it turned out, the fettuccine was quite good, and she laughed when he ate the entire portion, except for the mouthful he twirled into a nice little bundle and fed her, exhorting her to open wide, no, wider still. Even as he placed it in her mouth, a little of the sauce escaped to her upper lip. He took his napkin and carefully doctored the spill as he held her cheek with his other hand. She allowed him to baby her.

After this little expression of intimacy, Robert noticed that he remained close to her and that she didn't move away. Contrary to the thrust and parry of their earlier conversation, now they were laughing and talking about something they both loved—food.

She admitted a weakness for champagne and caviar. He confessed his predilection for foie gras, from Strasbourg, if at all possible. Her favorite dessert was anything with strawberries and heavy cream. He liked chocolate in any form. She lounged back in the booth, perfectly at ease. They were having a good time. In fact, he hadn't had such a good time in several years. Her company was intoxicating, and she wore a seductive scent of musky jasmine that drew him even closer to her. He couldn't take his eyes off her. His attention didn't faze her. She was enjoying her conquest.

He didn't speak of being a good cook, but obviously he'd had plenty of time to follow any number of interests wherever they led and to become expert at some. And if you're French, the culinary arts don't go unappreciated. He remembered Marie-Anne, a *cuisinière* whom his family had employed at their château near Orléans when he was a child. She was a roly-poly sort, a classic French peasant, but skilled by doing. Her knowledge wasn't found in books; it was the kind that was passed down through generations. Her mother and grandmother as well as her aunts had probably taken turns holding her when she was a baby as they stirred a pot in the kitchen. And since every foodstuff imaginable came from either the gardens or the fields or the woods surrounding the estate, her repertoire was wide and deep.

And in the 1700s, farm-to-table and eating locally and organically was a way of life. Robert hadn't begun to cook until after the Second

World War. Previously he had always been fortunate to have cooks and other household personnel to prepare meals and maintain his home. But there came a time when he reasoned that full-service personal staff can be intrusive, and they are rarely content to know just a little of your business but instead make it a point to know everything. As times changed and class distinctions and separations were reduced, he decided that privacy, indeed secrecy, was more important than the convenience and luxury of a staff of servants. Now he confined his households to a sole housekeeper each.

He must have been musing a little longer than he realized, because Alexis asked, "You must like Cole Porter."

"I do. How did you know?"

"Because you're humming the tune along with the piano."

"Well, at least I didn't break out in song." He was embarrassed.

"Do you know which song it is?"

"I'm guessing, but is it 'Let's Do It (Let's Fall in Love)'?"

"I doubt you're guessing."

Dinner wound down, and Robert glanced at the time—it was 9:30. There was the two-hour martini lunch and then there was the three-hour martini dinner. After the drinks and the bottle of wine, Robert was feeling relaxed and warm. Alexis didn't seem to be in a hurry, but when the waiter brought the check, the spell was broken.

They attempted to outdo each other declaring the evening a success, both mentioning aspects such as the food, the company, the conversation, and her cautioning against discounting the role of the martinis. But he didn't follow up with any proposition to make another date, and he knew that she wouldn't suggest anything without more of a commitment from him. There's checkers and then there's chess. Robert had a feeling that Alexis was a chess player.

The hotel valet brought her car first, a Bentley convertible of powder blue. *They must run in the family,* Robert thought. He saw her into her car, but before he closed the door, he leaned in and kissed her ever so lightly on the lips. She let him.

"Thank you for a lovely evening," she said. "Perhaps . . . It was a lot of fun."

"Yes, it was. Be careful. I'll see you soon."

The Bentley rolled down the incline of the hotel's driveway, stopping briefly at the corner. The light turned green, and she crossed Sunset. At the same time, the valet arrived with his car. He was home in three minutes. He could have walked.

Once in his garage, he entered the house through the side door that accessed a large gourmet kitchen furnished with all the most modern technological culinary equipment and gadgets. Robert had an antique collection of pots and pans as well as food-preparation tools and utensils, some dating back to his childhood. As a matter of fact, the whole house was demonstrative of the clash between modern and antique.

Robert and the decorator had battled in the beginning. Since the house was classic English Tudor, she wanted to carry out an English décor motif, but Robert dismissed that idea, much preferring the more modern and eclectic designs of Italian furniture. He was unperturbed that the exterior would be of one period while the inside would be in the style of a contemporary condo out of *Architectural Digest*. He found that the unexpected discovery of the modern interior spoke to his own evolution and acceptance of new things. It wouldn't suit him at all to retain everything that was past.

He was pleased with the way the house had turned out. But a large house can be lonely. Winding his way from the kitchen to the second-floor master suite, he turned the lights on then off as he made his way through the house, a vision of Alexis in his mind. She was nice, very nice, he told himself: a worrisome but pleasant serendipity.

And the next morning, the thought of her was still there rolling around in his mind, an engaging but disquieting plight. Alexis was not in the master plan. The plan, conceived after much deliberation back in Rome, dictated that Robert would come to Los Angeles and set up a comfortable life, establish a few one-dimensional relationships like the coffee klatch and perhaps a book club and a tennis membership, but otherwise he would avoid any situations that might promote anyone getting to know him better.

Alexis could have been a kind of ditzy astrologist cum tarot reader—in essence, a disorganized mess. With those characteristics, he wouldn't have thought twice about exploring a relationship with her. But ditzy she wasn't. On the contrary, she had probably at one time or another considered all the same philosophical forks in the road Robert had. In Robert's case, he had chosen the scientific method, the mathematical equation, and worshipped at the altar of empiricism. Alexis, with her education, had been exposed to all the advantages of the philosophy of the empiricists like Locke and Descartes, but apparently, where they had been the answer for Robert, she had continued on, insisting that rational thinking was insufficient to deal with the frailties and mysteries of being human.

This evidence of insistence and dogged curiosity made her a danger to Robert's secret. And he could never tell anyone, even if he were in love. He had already had to deal with mounting incredulity in his past relationships. And if the truth were known by a confidant or by a lover, could he expect the secret to be kept? If revealed, he could find himself the subject of study and experimentation at some university medical school, or worse, some government institution. He decided to give it a few days and see if a little separation would cool his interest and perhaps hers. Time was always an ally.

If not, it could lead to trouble.

FOUR

The next morning, he walked to Café Malmaison dreading Martin's anticipated inquisition camouflaged as rambling. He couldn't know how unnerving it was for Robert. Martin loved his daughter, and Robert guessed that he sensed he had found someone unique for his choosy offspring. But how could Robert accommodate his nosiness and not offend him or give away too much for him to report back to Alexis?

When Robert arrived, Martin was in his usual place, the chairman of the board. Thank God most of the group was already there—Alfred, E. W., Simon, and Lee. The others would drift in over the next half hour. The usual banter was in the air, but this morning's session would be abbreviated because E. W. had organized a golf game in a format he termed a "gangsome." It was a new word for Robert, but he understood that the number of players was a lot more than four. Before the hour was up, the duffers were on their way, leaving Martin and Robert by themselves. The safety in numbers was gone. How convenient for Martin.

"Heard you two were having martinis—my favorite—at the Polo Lounge," Martin said.

"Yes. We had a good time. Alexis is quite a woman. She's perfect," Robert said.

"She's too perfect. Hard to adjust to if you're a man, particularly if you're a Neanderthal like me."

"The Neanderthal seems well adjusted to Miss Mimi." Robert meant this comment as a tribute to them both.

"Mimi is entirely different."

"But cut from the same cloth."

"She likes you."

Robert noticed that Martin had crossed both his arms and legs. This was an unusual discussion to have about the daughter of a man in his sixties.

"I like Mimi too."

"No, Alexis. Mimi likes you too, though." Martin would not be distracted from his mission.

"How do you know?" He looked at his watch, indicating he needed to leave.

"She told me."

"I'm not sure she would like your betrayal of her confidence."

"There's no betrayal," he said, raising his voice for emphasis. "She told me to tell you."

Robert winced internally. Alexis was a lot smarter than even he had imagined. And she knew how to get her way. Martin was trained, already harnessed and saddled with a bit in his mouth. If Robert continued down this path, he would find himself as daunted as Martin.

"Well, you can tell her I like her, too."

"Why don't you two get together and just tell each other? I'm too old for this."

"We will, I'm sure, but I'm heading to New York on unexpected business."

"Alexis will be disappointed."

"I am, too."

Robert could see that Martin was let down. He'd probably planned for Alexis and Robert to continue to see each other more and more frequently until his shepherding was no longer required. He saw this unexpected interruption as quite possibly dousing the rising flame of passion. And that's precisely what Robert had in mind, both for his own passion as well as hers—if there was any. He didn't really want to go to New York, but he couldn't remain in town and take the chance that he might be caught in a lie. He didn't want to leave, period, but he needed some time and distance to think it through. He would leave the next day.

That afternoon, he was packing and taking care of some bill paying and correspondence with his bank in Zurich when his cell phone rang. He looked at the number. Alexis. Martin had been busy.

"*Robert?*" she asked. He guessed that was his new pet name.

"Hi, Alexis. I was just going to call you."

"No, you weren't. You let Martin tell me you were leaving."

"Not really."

"You don't have to run off to New York just to avoid a relationship with me."

"Where would you get that idea? I'm not doing anything of the sort."

"Just remember I'm the clairvoyant in this twosome, and I can clearly see that you're running away. I know that you're attracted to me, and you know that I like you. It's not a question of whether or not you are running away. It's why."

"I think you're overanalyzing. I'll call you when I get back."

"This is ridiculous," she said with some finality.

She was right. He didn't know what he should term her intuition, but it did border on clairvoyance, as he understood it. Was he the proverbial moth attracted to the flame? If he went to New York, he would probably lose her.

Against his better judgment, an hour later he called her back. She answered on the second ring, a good sign.

"Yes?" she answered.

"Why don't you come with me?"

***

Given the time difference between New York and L.A., he had decided that they should take an early-morning flight to arrive in time for dinner in the city. As it turned out, it was a good choice. They were in first class, side by side, and without any coaxing, Alexis found his shoulder very accessible to lean against and doze. He held her arm and hand, registering her softness and the relaxed breaths of her nap. They both dozed off, pleasantly connected in the most casual and comfortable of ways.

They arrived at LaGuardia Airport in Queens, New York, at five in the afternoon. A limousine took them into the city to the Four Seasons Hotel on East Fifty-Seventh Street. Robert had reserved a suite. Alexis in all likelihood knew New York a lot better than he did; he had come a few times on business, but she had been married to a New Yorker.

They were both adults, he a lot more adult than she knew, but the fact remained that the most intimacy they had shared was when he had wiped the fettuccine sauce from her upper lip. There was no way to stretch that to flirting or foreplay. They hadn't kissed beyond a peck. He guessed they had been about one date away from making love before he announced he was going to New York. And yet, in his experience, nearly all women were clairvoyant about sex. This could be awkward. He had thought about reserving two rooms, but what would that have indicated? No, one room was the only option.

"You don't need to be anxious about our sleeping together," she said. "I'll be gentle."

"That's good news. Would you like to go to Cipriani for dinner tonight?"

"It's been a long day. Would you mind if we had room service instead?"

Normally that would have been his suggestion. But she seemed a step ahead of him at each turn. They arrived and were shown to a gorgeous suite on a high floor. She looked around, surveying the view downtown as well as the furnishings and space, lots of it.

"I guess you might as well go first class. You can't live forever," she said.

He mumbled agreement and something about it being a nice room. They unpacked. He gave her the larger closet and even passed along the additional hangers from his closet. They planned to stay only three days, but she had brought two large suitcases, and he couldn't help but wonder what was in them: hats, shoes, handbags, all of the above?

"I think I'll take a quick shower and change," she said.

After forty-five minutes, she came out of the bathroom in an ivory-colored silk robe trimmed with aqua piping. Her dark hair was down at full length, well below her shoulders and slightly disheveled. He was certain that this was not a mistake. He wondered but didn't see any pant legs showing where the robe ended.

"Shorts," she said.

"Should we order and then I'll take my shower?"

"I'm in no hurry. Take your time, and then we'll order and have a glass of champagne."

Oui, madame, he thought, but of course her suggestion made more sense. He shaved, took a vigorous shower, and put on the hotel bathrobe. He hadn't brought any pajamas. He didn't own any pajamas.

When he came out, she looked at him, her gaze traveling down to where the bathrobe stopped.

"No shorts," he said.

"Breezy."

"Would you like some caviar?" he asked.

"Yes, caviar makes me feel sexy," she said.

Before they could reach the bed in the other room, he was all over her. She dropped the robe on the way, and the effect of the shorts was lost because he got rid of those along with the top as he eased her onto the bed. She meanwhile was busy loosening the tie of his bathrobe. When they weren't kissing and looking into each other's eyes, they were appreciating each other's assets. Their hands and mouths were busy. He took her all in, but there was such passion, pent up from their earlier arm's-length encounters, that they both knew extended foreplay would have to wait for another time. They each exerted pressure to indicate desire and egged each other on. Her movements and soft moans encouraged him to explore her most sensitive and intimate spots. Soon they were rocking back and forth, heading toward the ecstasy of fulfilled desire. They both knew how to stretch out what could have been over in a few minutes.

Holding her afterward seemed the most natural thing in the world. She nestled in a comfortable spot, cradled in his arms. He nuzzled her hair, grazing her ear, breathing deep sighs of satisfaction. After a time, she got up, naked and uncovered, and walked to the bathroom. A few minutes later, she came back. She had found one of his shirts.

They ordered caviar and toast points and a bottle of Taittinger Brut champagne, and for a change of taste, a bowl of fresh strawberries, two scoops of vanilla ice cream, and whipped cream. They turned out the lights and lit the two candles on the room-service table that had been rolled in. Robert searched through the Spotify selections and found some Charles Aznavour to intensify the mood. That Alexis spoke a little French and understood more pleased Robert.

"More caviar?" he asked with a mischievous but wry smile.

"I told you what it does to me."

"I can help you out with that," he said, taking her in his arms and pressing her against him.

"Would you?" She let him lead her toward the bedroom.

He rolled the room-service table into the hall and returned to find her in bed and his shirt on the floor. That was all he needed to know.

***

The next morning, they dressed in tracksuits and went down to the hotel dining room for breakfast. The Four Seasons was known for its power breakfasts, where men and women of high finance gathered to see and be seen as well as to meet their associates and competitors on neutral turf. The setting was grand, with wood paneling of a light color extending the entire height of the room, some forty feet. The furnishings were expensive, the furniture custom designed with an art deco aesthetic using various woods of deep and light colors and shiny blacks. Most of the hotel guests had breakfast in their room, but Robert liked the dining room and a brisk walk down Fifth or Madison Avenue afterward. Alexis was like-minded.

They ordered the healthy choice—Four Seasons granola, fresh fruit, a French yogurt, and dark-roast coffee. The croissants looked flaky and buttery, but they resisted. Afterward, they exited the hotel on the Fifty-Eighth Street side and proceeded up Madison Avenue hand in hand, stopping periodically to check out the boutique windows.

Robert noticed that the previous evening's activities hadn't altered their precoital relationship as he might have imagined. There was a mellowness presiding over their actions. There was always the chance that some form of buyer's remorse might set in, given how quickly things had developed. But no, they were on a different plane. When they returned to the hotel and were back in their room, he thought he might tackle the subject, but Alexis had her own ideas.

"I think I'll get a massage when you go to your appointment."

"Alexis. There is no appointment."

"No appointment?"

"I'm sorry. I lied to you."

"I presumed as much. Why do I frighten you?"

Now there was a question that couldn't be answered. She was either a good guesser or she was what she said she was. The thought was frightening.

"I haven't done this in a while."

"We're even. Neither have I."

***

Robert was glad to be in New York. In Manhattan, as in Rome or Paris, you walked, whereas in L.A. it was so spread out he normally ended up driving most places. And Alexis was in good shape, probably Pilates or yoga, so she was game for any suggestion, downtown, crosstown, plus she wore stylish but sensible shoes.

It was a beautiful day. Robert suggested a restaurant called San Pietro, which had outdoor seating, between Madison and Fifth. They took a table under one of the umbrellas. Robert ordered two Campari and sodas. San Pietro had the best olives and *grissini*, homemade bread sticks.

"Robert? Robert Valmer? I thought you had disappeared," said a tall man in a pinstriped dark-gray suit as he approached their table.

"Oh, hello, Jack. Let me introduce you to a friend of mine, Alexis Roth. Alexis, Jack Tillinghast," Robert said as he got to his feet.

Jack bowed his head slightly in deference to Alexis and then said, "What's it been? Five years? No, six; the last time was in Davos. Do you remember?"

"Of course, the conference. Yes, that was interesting."

"My God, Robert, you haven't changed a peg," Jack said. "How do you do it? Must be that Roman Frascati wine. Condolences about Arianna." Jack looked first at Robert, then Alexis, probably hoping he hadn't overstepped the line in mentioning Arianna.

"Thank you."

"How long are you in town?" Jack asked. "Maybe we could get together. Hey, I know. Tim, Tim Turnov. You remember him, Goldman Sachs? He would love to hear what you're doing these days. Still king of currency?"

"Unfortunately, I'm only here for a day or two, but maybe on the next trip. This was unexpected." If Jack stayed much longer, he might ask for a chair.

"Sure, just give me a call. You know where to find me." He nodded at Alexis. "Nice to meet you, Ms. Roth."

With Jack's departure, a silence ensued. Alexis was waiting for Robert to say something, probably a clarification as to exactly who Jack was. But he became too busy asking her if she would like to try some of the pappardelle with black truffles, ordering a bottle of a Tuscan Antinori, and discussing the vintage possibilities with the waiter to notice.

Finally she asked, "Who was that?"

"Jack Tillinghast, a commodities trader with UBS. I met him in Geneva a few years ago, and I've bumped into him at various financial conferences. He's a currency expert."

"You could visit with him and the other friend he mentioned if you want to."

"No, I'll see them some other time."

Lunch finished, they took the long way back to the hotel, going up and down the streets between Madison and Fifth, sometimes being enticed by the windows to explore the possibilities inside. The wine, the food, and whatever scent Alexis was wearing, that hint of jasmine, began to give him ideas. But when they got back to the hotel, she proposed that they get a massage. He passed, and she went ahead to the spa for a massage and a manicure. She was gone for three hours. And when she returned she went straight to the bathroom to get ready for dinner. An air of strangeness had intruded on the proceedings.

As they settled in at Nello on Madison, Robert decided to tread lightly but deftly. "Is something wrong?"

"Yes. I'm trying to adjust to the fact that I'm attracted to you, and yet I know so little about you. It bothers me because my instincts tell me that there's a limit to what you intend to let me know about you."

"I thought I had answered your every question." He motioned for the waiter.

"Am I supposed to get to know you through interrogation?"

"I'm sorry you feel that way." He pointed to a Brunello on the list. Anything to make the conversation more casual.

"But I do, and I believe with some justification."

"I'm not sure I can be different than I am." He hoped his expression indicated a desire for mercy.

"For some reason, I think it's more than that."

"Are you relying on your feelings or your professional training?"

"Both," she said rather ominously.

"So, where do we go from here?" he asked with some despair. This was not the talk of lovers but rather a discussion between two people, at least one of whom was expressing a grievance.

"It's uncertain. You're not reassuring me that you'll be more forthcoming. Perhaps you can't. And I can't be with anyone, no matter how attractive, if they're not honest."

"What can I say?"

"If there was something, you would have already said it. You either can't or won't."

He didn't get much sleep that night, and Alexis didn't either, but they didn't speak. They tossed and turned on their own as if they were in separate beds, if not separate rooms.

The night seemed to go on forever and yet ended too quickly. They were so close yet so far apart, and he feared that this might be the end of their relationship.

FIVE

Arriving back in L.A. midafternoon, Robert dropped Alexis off at her condominium. It was all very cordial. There wasn't any bickering or pouting. And they actually talked on the plane, but all subjects related to their relationship were off limits, and they both respected the agreed-upon but unspoken rules. She allowed him to give her a kiss on both cheeks. They both professed the idea that they would see each other soon. Then he was back home, alone and disappointed and knowing full well that it was his fault.

But what could he do about it? She was what he wanted in almost every way save one, but it was unlikely that she would enter a relationship where any secrets were kept. True, he had only one secret to keep, but its nature precipitated a labyrinth of lies and omissions. This was what she had picked up on. And how could he solve that for her?

Monday came and Robert decided to skip Café Malmaison, knowing that Martin would be poised to find out exactly what had happened. And Alexis apparently didn't have many secrets from her father, so he would know all about their failed getaway. Instead he decided to walk around the neighborhood. In one way it was strange that he cared about health and fitness. He'd never had reason to see a doctor, and he couldn't risk a checkup—who knew what some of their panel of tests might reveal. He hadn't been ill in years except for an occasional case of the sniffles. He did gain five pounds here and there, but he was always able to shed those add-ons by watching what he ate for a week or two.

Instead, he walked up to Sunset then down to North Palm, then down to Santa Monica and back to Rodeo. It took him around forty minutes since he wasn't power walking, just meandering along. As he approached his driveway, he saw Martin's Bentley at the curb in front of his house. Martin was sitting in the car. Clearly, he wouldn't be denied.

Robert tapped on the passenger side window. Martin unlocked the car door, and Robert opened it.

"We missed you this morning," Martin said with the look of a person who had more on his mind than Robert's truancy.

"I was a little tired," Robert said, perhaps not very believably.

"I always go for a long walk when I'm tired."

"I don't want to talk about it."

"With me or her?" Martin asked, impatience rising in his voice.

"Neither."

"You two are acting like children," Martin said in a tone of disgust. His rather large hands and fingers pressed in a steeple.

"I know."

"What's next?"

"Are you the local yenta?"

"I'm a busybody, nosing into everything." Now Robert understood Martin's wringing of his hands and steepling of his fingers. He was nervous.

"That explains it."

"Call her. Don't be an ass. Apologize and promise to do better. It always works for me."

With those parting words, Martin drove away. Under normal circumstances he would be right. But even if he and Alexis talked it through and he apologized and promised to be more forthcoming, would it be enough? Or would she always suspect or expect more and then more still? Why couldn't they just enjoy what they had, which was quite a lot in his estimation? No, she wouldn't be satisfied unless he could be more open about his past. She wanted it all.

A possible solution would be for him to amalgamate experiences from several different time frames—his student days, interactions with his father, his brief residence in Geneva, and then the more recent times in Rome. He just had to compress his life into a story with a much shorter time span. There were enough stories to fill his stated forty-eight years several times over. All he had to do was to pick the right episodes and keep straight what he had told her before. He could do this by always telling the truth, only changing the time frame.

Maybe he should wait a few days. Maybe she could find a reason to be less demanding. *Better to wait it out and see what happens,* he told himself. "Oh, *merde,*" he said aloud, dialing her number.

He received the "in session" response and left a message asking her to return his call.

An hour later, his cell phone rang. "You called?" she said.

"Your father told me to." He thought that was funny. She didn't.

"What's on your mind?"

"You. I was wondering if I could make an appointment. I feel like I need a session with Dr. Roth."

"You need a session with Dr. Ruth."

"Can we get together later and have dinner? I think we should talk."

"Come over to my place at six. Then we'll decide whether we should have dinner."

***

One of the building's concierge staff announced his arrival and escorted him to a bank of elevators and selected the floor using a security fob. When the elevator stopped on twenty-eight, the doors opened, and he was already in her condominium. Alexis was sitting on a large white sofa, and beyond her were floor-to-ceiling windows spanning the entire length of the room, providing a spectacular view from the Hollywood sign all the way to Catalina. They embraced, and she offered him a glass of white wine that he readily accepted. It was a California Chardonnay, Far Niente, and a good one.

"I'm very fond of you," he began, "but you know that. Can we start again?"

"Will it be any different?"

"I can only try. What do I need to do?"

"I want to know who you are. You're very, very . . . I don't know what, but you're not generous with personal information. It makes me uneasy. It makes me think you have something to hide."

"I'm modest. I'm French. We're restrained."

"No, it's not that. When I ask you a question, you answer, but it's an answer devoid of details. You must have a lot of practice deflecting."

"I'm not conscious of it."

"That doesn't make any difference to someone who's trying to like you more."

"Perhaps I can't be someone I'm not."

"I have a proposition. Let's give it a few weeks, a month. I'll try to accept your reticence, and you try to be more open. We'll have dinner, we'll have lunch, we'll have sex, and we'll see."

And this is how they began dating again. They had dinner, they had sex, and they had breakfast. And he did what he could on the openness front. He decided it was OK to speak of the last twenty-five years or so. Robert found that Alexis either didn't want to know or was not interested in his former wife, Arianna, but she, like most Americans, enjoyed hearing about his professional life as a currency trader. It was a field that Alexis knew nothing about, but she was curious. When he followed the new rules of being more expansive, she listened attentively while he described puts and calls, derivatives, arbitrage, and gold futures. He even threw in a few specific incidents regarding hedges that he had made about currencies connected with certain unstable governments in South America and Africa.

The renewal was going smoothly until one Saturday when they had spent a lot of time together. They had already been to lunch and were back at her condo. It had been three weeks since their grand bargain, and she still hadn't been over to his house.

"I've been reading up on some French history," she said.

"What period?"

"On the prerevolutionary and revolutionary period. I've been particularly interested in one Count de Valmer. He had a son, also Robert de Valmer. The de Valmer property and château were near Orléans. When was the *de* dropped?"

"I'm not sure there's any connection."

"I saw a painting of the son. I think he was twenty-six at the time."

"And where would you find something like that?"

"There are multiple sites on the Internet tracing aristocratic families from European countries, the heraldry, and some even show paintings and photographs. Did you know that Robert de Valmer looks like you, only younger?"

"The Valmer genes are strong, I guess."

"Must be. It's eerie," she said.

And this was the kind of situation that she had been talking about, where his natural inclination kicked in to try and pass something off, to not follow the drift of the conversation but to see if it would die where it was. But he also had the feeling that this wouldn't die that easily, so he jumped in.

"I remember that my grandfather's name was Edouard and my father's name was Robert. And the *de* was not part of either of their names. I didn't know that I had another ancestor named Robert." He hoped that this information would demonstrate enough enthusiasm.

"There was a cousin, too, and his name was Philippe. He was killed in Paris by a street mob at the beginning of the French Revolution," Alexis said.

Robert flinched at the mention of Philippe, the memory coming back unbidden. He and Philippe had escaped the mob, but the wound inflicted on his cousin by the brick was more serious than originally thought. He died two days later. The doctor that had been called in said it was probably a blood clot on the brain due to a traumatic concussion. And he was only thirty-two years old. He and Robert had been inseparable. Philippe's mother, Robert's aunt, the one they had been sent to rescue, was inconsolable. And to make matters worse,

Philippe's father, the brother of Robert's father, was guillotined a month later.

"Perhaps that's why the *de* was dropped."

"I find family history fascinating. And it's important in my work to understand people."

"I can see that. My father was a very private person, even distant." Robert smiled. "Now you can psychoanalyze me with that tidbit."

"It explains a lot."

Robert thought he had acquitted himself rather well under the circumstances, and he hadn't felt uncomfortable telling her what he did. Most of it was true. That was the easy part. The hard part was keeping the real truth about Robert de Valmer secret. Either Alexis decided that he'd had enough for this session or that was as far as her investigation had taken her. Time would tell which one was the case.

SIX

Now that they were a regular couple, and they had managed several weeks of peaceful coexistence, Robert thought it might be time to invite Alexis over to his place. She had turned down his first invitation, all those weeks ago. Perhaps it was time to invite her again.

He called her early on Sunday morning. Their new arrangement was progressing well enough that they planned further in advance than just the next date. Alexis seemed happy and wasn't pressing him as much as in the beginning. Still . . .

The only problem was that her practice occupied much of her time; she was fielding calls at all hours from what he supposed were anxious and entitled clients who sought her counsel and reassurance. These calls were confidential and demanded privacy. He had become adept at leaving the room or excusing himself when these interruptions came. He didn't ask her about her clients, and there were no leaks. From time to time, articles appeared in the various gossip rags, even sometimes creeping into the *L.A. Times*, and these left little doubt as to her clientele. And her regulars weren't confined to movie and TV stars; he saw that she coached several of the leading producers and directors as well as some of the moneymen in the entertainment industry.

Robert could see how her former bicoastal marriage might have suffered from her dedication to her work. It was more than work; it was a passion, and one that would compete with all other interests. In some ways, her focus on her clients gave him some relief from being in the spotlight. Alexis didn't tolerate things being out of place, and he knew that, regarding him, there were very troubling things out of place. She didn't state what needed tidying up, but he was certain that, from her perspective, not all the files were in the correct drawer.

That day, she answered, and he said, "Alexis, *mia mela*. Let's cook something at my house tonight. We can go to the farmers' market this morning and buy the *nécessités*."

"I'd better not find out that *mia mela* means chubby," she said.

"Of course not. The free translation is 'apple of my eye.' Italians love apples."

"Italians love to pinch girls' bottoms."

"They like that, too. They're not mutually exclusive."

The Beverly Hills farmers' market was open early every Sunday between the streets of Rexford and Crescent, next to the public library just off Santa Monica. Robert had ventured there a couple of times previously just to see what all the fuss was about. He was surprised to see that the produce and other comestibles compared favorably with European street markets in the quality and diversity of their offerings. It wasn't the market in Aix-en-Provence, but it was more than passable.

Alexis picked him up, and they drove over and parked on Foothill a couple of blocks away. Robert complimented her choice of grocery-shopping attire. She had donned a Roberto Cavalli warm-up, a black number with a raging gold serpent on the back embroidered in multiple colors, for the occasion. The pants showed off a gold stripe on the outside of each leg, the front a black calfskin while the back of the trouser was black jersey. She also sported a pair of Zanotti gold high-tops.

"You look good in Roberto Cavalli," he said.

"Thanks, but how is it that you know so much about fashion, even the designers?"

"I lived in Italy, and I'm French. We pay attention."

"There must be more, knowing you."

"OK. At one time I participated in financing a number of designers in Florence and Rome. I became interested because I wanted to make sure my money was being spent prudently."

"It wasn't only currency trading?"

"Mostly, but sometimes I dabbled in other things." She seemed to process it all and didn't have any follow-up questions.

Alexis was in a gay mood. Inviting her over and going grocery shopping had been a good idea. She was enthusiastic, asking him what they were going to cook.

"How about a nice *loup de mer*, a Mediterranean sea bass?"

"I don't cook fish," she said.

"You don't cook fish, or you don't clean fish?"

"Neither."

"You're in luck. I do both."

They did a once-through of the market and got their bearings, came up with a plan of action, and then made a final pass for the purchases. First the fish, a whole *loup de mer* of three pounds, more than enough for the two of them. Then the herbs—a few dried fennel twigs and fresh rosemary—and on to the dairy vendors and freshly churned butter from a *crémerie* in Ojai. They needed a vegetable, so Alexis opted for zucchini, and he selected some russet potatoes for roasting. For dessert, the most important stage in the meal, he proposed a gratinée of fresh berries.

"And who's preparing that?" she asked.

"*Moi.*"

He wanted to bargain with all the vendors, but after the fishmonger negotiations, where Robert was able to reduce the cost by 20 percent, Alexis persuaded him to pay full price for the rest.

"We always haggle in Europe. It's part of the fun," he said.

"It's not fun for the vendors. You have the upper hand. You have the money."

And she was right, but he did have a lot of experience in the haggling domain.

When they arrived back at his house and had put away the groceries, he noticed that she was looking at all the cooking utensils, some stored in large ceramic jars and others hanging from racks over the stove and sinks.

"You have quite a collection. Some of these look very old," she said.

"It's almost a fetish with me. Many are antique, not to be used, but they make great conversation pieces."

"They do. What is this?" she asked, pointing at one.

"That's a bean stringer. Never know when you might need one."

"And this?"

"A chestnut knife. Tough little nuts, they are."

"Weren't you disappointed by my kitchen?"

"Not with you in it."

Passing from the kitchen toward the main rooms of the house, she wanted to stop in the dining room, where there were cabinets upon cabinets with interior lights and glass fronts and mirrored backs. They were filled with china and serving dishes.

"If I need a plate, I know who to ask. What is all this?"

"I collect antique china services. Some are very old. Some are very chipped."

"This is not usually the domain of a man."

"We French have a passion for everything connected with food. Food is the next best thing to sex."

"You forgot air. But why so many?"

"When I get started at something, I don't know when to stop. Besides, each setting has its own unique utility, its own function. See, like this one, it's for fish soup, not bouillabaisse." He pointed at another. "This one's for bouillabaisse. Here's a service for cheese, and one for tea with all the little sandwich plates. And then there are the seasons to consider and whether the party is inside or is it a garden party or at the beach, formal, informal, one for wild game. It never ends."

"They're beautiful. Are they all French?"

"Most are French, but I have some great pieces over here that are Meissen. Actually, some of the German pieces are among the most valuable. They're not for the dishwasher."

They continued to the living room, or as he termed it, the great room, at the front of the house, which had a cathedral ceiling. The décor announced that it was a man's abode. Low-slung sofas and generous armchairs with comfortable and inviting upholstery distributed in an interesting arrangement, a dominating fireplace of black marble and what looked to be lava rocks, two walls of bookcases that stretched from floor to ceiling, filled with thousands of books. Modern lighting fixtures combined with indirect lighting gave a soft glow, and several paintings in prominent locations completed the look of the room.

"Is that a Pissarro?" she asked, moving closer to the Paris still life.

"It is." He liked that she knew what she was looking at.

"You didn't tell me you were a collector."

"One painting doesn't make me a collector."

"But the Braque over the desk does."

He wouldn't be able to fool her.

"That's a concert grand piano. Do you play?"

"A little. Would you like to see upstairs?" he asked, hoping to avoid a request to play.

"Is the bedroom upstairs?"

"Yes."

"I'd rather have some champagne first."

A big smile broke out across his face. "You have such great ideas."

"They're your ideas. I just say them out loud." She ran her fingers through her hair in a slow and sensuous manner.

There was nothing like a bottle of Krug to christen whatever the occasion. Before the bottle was finished, she had agreed to sit in his lap. He unzipped her warm-up jacket. He kissed her. She took off her shoes. He kissed her again.

"Want to have that look upstairs now?" he said.

"You're so subtle."

***

When they came back downstairs, the sun was just slipping beneath the horizon, providing that glow somewhere between soft yellow and gold that only occurs in Los Angeles. Robert set up the kitchen to cook the meal the way a chef would for prep. Alexis took one of the stools and sat watching him as he readied the fish for the grill. Then he washed the potatoes, doused them with oil, salt, and rosemary, placed them in a copper roasting pan, and slid them into the bottom oven. He peeled the zucchini and cut them into medium-sized *allumettes*—matchsticks.

"Sauté is OK for the zucchini, or do you prefer steamed?" Robert asked.

"You're really good at this. Sauté is fine."

Then she saw him quickly mix the flour, butter, almond flour, and cream as the base for the fresh-berry gratin. It was all coming together at just the right time. He had already set the table: fish plates, informal, outdoor, on the patio just off the kitchen. He checked the fish on the grill—it would be another two minutes. The zucchini required only a short time, and the potatoes issued forth from the oven a little crunchy on the outside, still soft on the inside. He opened a rosé from Domaine Ott, near Saint-Tropez, and dinner was served.

Alexis took her first bite of the *loup de mer*, lightly infused with the faint hint of burning twigs of fennel he had added to the fire at the last minute, and said, "Wolfgang Puck would be jealous."

"It's really nothing, my dear."

"No, really. It's not that you can cook. It's the way you prepare and use the utensils. I saw you peel and cut that zucchini. You're no amateur. And you play the piano."

"Badly."

"No one buys a concert-quality piano and plays badly. You play classical?"

"That, too, but I prefer show tunes."

"Cole Porter, as I recall. Where did you find the time to learn all these things?"

"I don't know. If you're interested in something, you can find the time."

After dinner they sat looking at the fire he had lit in the fireplace. It wasn't really cold enough for a fire, so he left the door slightly ajar. Romance trumped comfort. Robert could tell that Alexis was processing the events of the day. And this was the risk of letting her see Robert Valmer in his element. But he didn't anticipate her question.

"I can't understand why you're not more interested in your own lineage," she said with a curious frown. "You have all these collections, most of them antiques, yet you hardly care about your own family's roots."

"I didn't say I wasn't interested, but how far back should I go, and what would be the point?"

"I know my history," she said, her head up, her chest out. She was clearly proud of her knowledge. "It gives me great pride and solace to have it stored in my memory. It makes me who I am."

"Tell me about it."

"The Marans are an old Romanian Jewish family. My grandfather and grandmother, Yoel and Alma Marans, were either lucky or smart. They emigrated from Romania, Bucharest, sometime in 1934. He was a doctor and she was a musician, a cellist. They were very young, newly married. There had always been persecution of the Jews in Romania, and they decided to go to France, where they had relatives. But they stayed just long enough to obtain passage out of Brest to New York. That's where my father was born. My mother's heritage is Russian, Kiev, but she, too, was born in New York of immigrant parents. Martin and Mimi met in New York but moved to Los Angeles, where my father was a real estate investor. He still is. The Marans that stayed behind in Romania were all lost in the Holocaust. The plight of Romanian Jews is often overlooked in the history of World War II and the atrocities of the Third Reich. And that's the abbreviated version."

"I can understand, with so much loss, particularly given the circumstances, why you would want to learn all you could about your family," he said. "In my case, I don't have the same urgency."

She seemed to accept his explanation of limited interest, but at times she was hard to read. Whether it was calculated or not, Robert couldn't know. Her musings about her own family's history were

one thing, but when she drifted quite naturally over into tidbits of
fact that she had collected about his, it promoted the odd effect in
him of coaxing him to think more about his own past, making him
cautious and hesitant—the very qualities that were dangerous to their
relationship. He wished that she would learn enough to be satisfied,
but that wasn't the nature of her curiosity. She learned a little bit, and
that only spurred her to know more. Her nature was to burrow and
burrow like a mole, not knowing exactly what she was looking for
until finally bumping into her quarry in the dark. And this was exactly
what happened with Robert that evening.

***

The next morning—Alexis had stayed over—she was up and dressed
at an ungodly hour. *What's the rush?* he wondered. He was thinking
of a French breakfast. He expressed this sentiment with a degree of
surprise and disappointment.

"But *Robert*, some of us must work. I have just enough time to get
back to the condo and re-dress and get to the office for my ten o'clock
appointment."

"You need to move some emergency clothes over here. Make life
simple." He moved toward the closet, indicating a space for whatever
she might bring.

"Maybe you should move some things over to my place," she
countered.

"Is that an invitation?"

"Did you know you were talking in your sleep last night?"

"No. What did I say?" He looked the other way to try and regain
his composure.

She smiled mischievously. "I'll never tell."

"Oh, come on, don't be coy."

"Why, are you worried?"

He glanced at her, saw the amused look on her face. She was
enjoying his discomfort. "Of course not. What did I say?"

"Let's talk about it tonight. I've got to hurry." She was still smiling, but it wasn't that funny to Robert.

He had to let it go. If he asked her again, she would make more out of it than he would want. He had no idea that he talked in his sleep. No one had ever mentioned it before. Could she be baiting him? But what he might have said, and more important, how much he had said, and how intelligible it was, could determine how big the problem might be. After all, wasn't she the interpreter of dreams? Was she the interpreter of nightmares, too?

During the day, he continued to think about what he might have said. And as he thought it over, he ventured a guess that all that talk about family history the evening before had probably released some memory or anxiety in his subconscious. And when he was asleep, his unconscious had probably run wild, his memories taking full license to reenact events. And if he knew enough to put this together, then Alexis would be able to as well. But did the fact that she refused to tell him what he'd said mean that she was mulling over *how* to tell him or *how much* to tell him?

She called him that afternoon. "Are you coming over this evening?"

"Is that an invitation?"

"You do want to find out what you were talking about in your sleep, don't you?"

"Not really. I mutter a lot. Doesn't mean anything."

"That's what you think."

Later in the evening, after dinner, they were having a glass of wine while cuddling on the sofa, looking out over the expansive view toward Santa Monica. Up to that point, Alexis hadn't mentioned what was paramount on his mind, and he wondered what she was waiting for.

His patience was rewarded because she made no introduction, instead launching right in. "Who is Henri?"

"I don't know any Henris," he said, raising his voice, hoping he had said it with some conviction.

"Well, last night you did."

"Oh, you mean when I was muttering."

"No, it was quite clear. *No, no, Henri, I'm sorry.* It was all in French, but I think I got it right. *Regret* is 'sorry,' isn't it?" She looked at him questioningly.

"I still don't know any Henri."

"You just don't remember. You must have known someone named Henri, and it must have been a bad experience. You were shouting and sobbing." She was warming up to the interrogation, her clues coming in fast succession, one after another.

"Maybe I read a book or saw a movie that I remembered." He surprised himself at how quickly he was coming up with rational alternatives, but she was having none of it.

"No, not at all. My experience tells me that for this kind of intensity, it had to be something quite relevant to your life."

"Then why don't I remember it?"

"Maybe it's suppressed. Maybe you don't want to remember it."

"Everyone has things they would like to forget." Robert usually said this as a catchall; it was his subject-ending summation. Unfortunately, the workings of the mind and subconscious were Alexis's expertise, and he could see that she was interested in pursuing an answer, particularly one that appeared to be a mystery even to him.

"That's true, but the more we want to forget, the more firmly planted the event is in our memory. The subconscious doesn't fret over trivial matters."

This new development threatened to undo all the trust that had been created by his openness. He couldn't imagine that she would just let this go. She was too intelligent, too aware, and mostly too persistent. These were the same qualities, along with her beauty and personality, that made her irresistible. But if he was going to blab in his sleep, then how could they remain lovers? And if not lovers, how could they be friends?

"I know someone who is an expert on dreams, if you're interested in finding out what it means," she said.

"I thought you were the expert."

"I am, but I can't be your lover *and* your shrink."

"It's happened before." He hoped that the relief he felt that she was not to be his therapist wasn't obvious.

"Not with me it hasn't."

"You're too strict." He let out a chuckle when he said this.

"This is not a joking matter."

"I talked in my sleep, and you want me to go to therapy?"

"It's not the first time." Now she was doing her deep dive, really homing in. Her choice of words and telling him that it wasn't the first episode was obviously meant as both a surprise and perhaps a little "gotcha" as well.

"I've talked in my sleep before?"

"Yes, but last night was different. More like a nightmare."

Now what was he going to do? If he had talked in his sleep before, then what might he say in the future? She said it was in French, so perhaps she hadn't understood, but he knew exactly what all this was about, and she was right.

Some experiences can't be forgotten.

SEVEN

If there was one name Robert didn't need to mention in his sleep, or at any other time, it was Henri. Henri Louis Clement, to be precise. The Henri incident had precipitated the reason he had been forced to leave his beloved France for the second time in twenty-seven years.

Robert had met Henri in 1817 at the Bourse, the Paris stock exchange, two years after he had returned from exile in Switzerland after the French Revolution. They were both investors and traders—Robert in gold and currencies, Henri in government bonds. Henri was in his early thirties and came from an established mercantile family in Amiens, a town some seventy miles due north of Paris, and had the good fortune to have avoided serving in Napoleon's army. This enabled him to escape being categorized with the scores of young and middle-aged men associated with Napoleon's defeat and the devastating remunerative consequences that the allies had placed on France after Waterloo.

With Napoleon's exile and the return of the Bourbon dynasty in France, young men like Henri had been able to advance at a much quicker pace, in whatever their specialty, as the competition had been seriously depleted. These were the same set of facts that had also enabled Robert to return to France. He had been forced to leave during the French Revolution just after Philippe's and his uncle's deaths. Although the de Valmers weren't nobles in the truest sense, not participating in the court at Versailles, they were still Royalists, meaning that they had sided with the king and their titles were derived from royal decrees. For them, there was no choice. If the forces of change achieved their aims, the de Valmers had a lot to lose. When Louis XVI was guillotined in early 1793, Robert and his father had escaped to Zurich, where his father later died, exiled, bitter, and depressed.

Robert Valmer was already an established fixture on the Paris Bourse when Henri first came on the scene. He was brash and eager and ambitious, and he soon made a name for himself at the recently renovated stock exchange in the first arrondissement. He was handsome and debonair and newly rich, far richer than when he had arrived in Paris some three years earlier. Youth and exuberance fueled by success had promoted a reckless approach in his financial speculation, where he often bought bonds of countries either involved in war or on the verge of war. Naturally his mounting fame and renowned invincibility regarding his wagers—and they couldn't be termed more politely— created jealousies among his colleagues and an infatuation among Parisian women of high ambition and low ethics.

Complimented, Henri took all this fawning to mean that he himself was irresistible to women and that his particular circumstance of wealth had nothing to do with their swoon. Those who were of his long line of consecutive consorts did nothing to dissuade him from holding himself in the highest regard. And the more he became convinced of his inordinate power, the more a resulting destructive pride caused him to demand a respect from his associates and friends, one that was disproportionate to reality.

Robert had first met him on the floor of the exchange. Sometimes they were competitors, and sometimes they were allies. Robert decided early on to avoid auctions where they might confront each other directly. He loved Henri's enthusiasm, and he was amusing to watch as he bested his friends and charmed his foes. Like Henri, Robert enjoyed the company of women, and if accompanied by a friend who was of the same predilection, the game of looking for a woman was played with the same passion as that of shaving a quarter of a point off an asking price. Henri loved winning in all categories. And the root cause of Robert's disastrous clash with Henri wasn't money, but a woman.

"Excuse me. Remember me? I'm still here," Alexis said as she waved her hand in front of Robert's face to break his trance.

"Oh, sorry, I was thinking about your suggestion," Robert said.

"Or were you thinking about Henri?"

"Nonsense. What's her name?" Robert knew where this had to end up if he were to continue seeing Alexis.

"Sorry, my darling, it's a he," she said.

"And I presume you have a working relationship with this person."

She frowned in mock disgust. "I know him quite well, but your therapy would be strictly confidential between you and him. He was one of my professors at Stanford—Aaron Mendelssohn."

"Is he a musician?" He smiled. She didn't.

"Don't be funny. Do you want me to contact him?"

"Where's he located?"

"On Bedford. You can walk."

"Let me think about it."

"I've been around long enough to know what that means," she said. She was doing everything but tapping her foot in impatience.

"I've been around quite a while myself. I'll think about it."

He had a difficult choice to make. If he did nothing, then he might continue to talk in his sleep. And he had recently seen an Alliance Française French conversation primer lying on Alexis's nightstand. That meant that she was trying to improve her French. Although from what she said, he spoke uniquely in French when he talked in his sleep, he couldn't count on her patience with his nocturnal babble or that she ultimately wouldn't understand enough to begin to piece the puzzle together.

A day or two after—they hadn't spent the night together since her recommendation that he seek therapy—he acquiesced and told her she could contact Dr. Mendelssohn. The following night, she told him that the referral had been made, and he could call and make an appointment.

"Did you preview Dr. M on why I was coming?" he asked.

"Of course not. That would be unethical."

Robert wondered if he could indeed count on the ethics of these two long-term friends. Or would one or the other be seeking out reasons to compare notes, perhaps dropping little hints and innuendos regarding him? He had learned over his life that trusting people to do the right thing was a poor bet. More often people would serve their own interests and then rationalize the breach of their ethics for a reason of overriding importance.

There was one thing he needed to admit to himself if not Alexis. And that was that he had fallen in love with her. How could he have resisted? And if he wasn't in love with her, then he wouldn't risk exposure of his secret. Perhaps it was time for him to tell her he loved her before he immersed himself in therapy. His hope was that the good doctor could help him stop talking in his sleep without touching upon the truth, while Alexis surely hoped that he would discover the meaning behind his slips. He guessed that it might be possible for the doctor to intercede. After all, psychiatrists were experts on the subconscious, but whether he could do something without Robert's full participation was another matter. But if Robert didn't agree to see him, then Alexis would assume he had something to hide, which of course he did.

***

A week later he was in Dr. Mendelssohn's office. And Alexis was right, he could have walked, but he didn't. He went by car, since he and Alexis had made a date for lunch after his appointment. The office was on the fifth floor, the top floor of a modern office building in the heart of Beverly Hills. It was a medical building, and doctors of one specialty or another occupied all the suites.

Dr. M's office was well furnished with antique furniture, watercolors, a Persian carpet, and a copious supply of magazines on art and sculpture. Robert was the only person in the waiting room other than the receptionist, a middle-aged woman of few words. The doctor would be with him in a few minutes, he was told, and the first session would last for an hour and fifteen minutes, which would include the familiarization preface, but in the future, forty-five minutes would be the norm. While he waited, he filled out the health questionnaire. He was in good health, so most of his answers were negative.

Perhaps everyone had a picture in his head of what an airline pilot should look like, and anyone seeing a psychiatrist knows what a psychiatrist should look like. Dr. Aaron Mendelssohn appeared exactly as he should. A man probably in his mid-sixties—a few inches short of six feet, balding on top, with penetrating eyes, a gray suit, a light-blue shirt, and a tie the color of Bordeaux wine—rose from his desk as Robert entered his office. He shook Robert's hand—his skin was soft—and asked him to sit on the sofa while he sat in a large armchair just to one side.

"Thank you for arranging to see me on short notice. Alexis gives you the highest marks," Robert said.

"Alexis is special. You two are friends, I guess?" he said.

"Yes, good friends." Robert shifted uncomfortably on the sofa, wondering how much detail Alexis had shared.

"Can you tell me why you have come to see me?" He sounded genuinely concerned, much like a priest might inquire about a confession.

"Besides the fact that Alexis thought you might be able to help me, I have learned from an impeccable source that I talk in my sleep, and sometimes in a very agitated fashion."

"And what do you say?" If the doctor did know something, he wasn't about to let it escape his lips.

"I don't know what I say, but it was related to me that I speak in French—that's normal, I'm French—and the only word that was clearly understood by my source is 'Henri.' I say Henri."

"Does the source know any French?"

"No, but I believe she's working on it, though my experience tells me that it could take a while." Robert presumed that hint might release the doctor from any professional ethics of nondisclosure. He had to know that it was Alexis herself.

"I see. Then the only possibility is for you to work at unlocking your subconscious, which seems eager to get out during your sleep. But I forgot to ask, who is Henri?"

"I don't know."

"I presume you've searched your memory, including your earliest childhood memories, and have not located an Henri anywhere?"

"Yes, no luck."

"I guess we can assume that since *Henri* is French for Henry, the first clue is that it must have something to do with France. At some time in your life, someone named Henri must have made an impression of lasting consequence on your psyche. It's very strange that you can't remember anything. Perhaps it was an event with enough gravity that you have suppressed it."

"That's what Alexis said." Now there would be no doubt as to who the source was, but the wise doctor didn't blink.

"Alexis was one of my brightest students."

"She amazes me daily." And it was true. Robert wondered how he might fare against the tag team of Alexis and Dr. M.

"Have you ever undergone hypnosis?"

"No." For whatever reason, Robert could feel a little color spreading across his face.

Dr. M continued to ask his questions, and Robert continued to answer him truthfully, with the exception of admitting who Henri was. They agreed to meet the next week. In the meantime, the doctor recommended that he continue to rummage around for the identity of Henri.

Robert was fifteen minutes late for his lunch with Alexis. She had made the reservation in the garden at Spago, which was convenient to her office. The staff all knew her. She was already at a table on the terrace, under the shade of a large white canvas umbrella.

"Hi, my darling. He must like you. He never goes over," Alexis said, turning first one cheek and then the other, allowing him the double French greeting.

"He didn't say one way or the other," Robert said as he slid into a chair at a right angle to hers.

"We don't need to talk about it at all," she said.

"It's all right. He was as confused as I am. He didn't have many answers for me."

"You have all the answers. It's a matter of allowing them to bubble to the surface."

"Speaking of bubbles, how about some champagne?" He needed a drink.

"You French think champagne is the answer to everything."

"Not at all. But it is the answer to ninety-nine questions out of a hundred."

"That's what I mean."

You can't be hypnotized if you don't want to be, can you? That was the question Robert kept circulating in his mind. He could fend off Dr. M through equivocation and the pretense of ignorance or of not remembering, but if he were hypnotized, then he might reveal what he didn't want to. But all eyes, at least those of Dr. M and Alexis, were on him. He was the key to deciphering this mysterious reference to Henri.

It wasn't as if he had murdered Henri, but he *had* killed him. And he hadn't died immediately. Death had come after three agonizing days, a combination of blood loss and infection. It had all been so unnecessary, so foolish and so tragic. And that was the reason Robert sometimes woke up in a panic, sweat permeating the sheets and pillows. At least that hadn't happened when he was with Alexis. Maybe his subconscious was smarter than he thought.

And what else but jealousy and pride over a woman could precipitate such a tragedy between two friends? The tragic truth was that a misunderstanding had planted the seed of mistrust that would ultimately end Henri's life and require Robert's exile from France. How different it could have been had Henri had not been such a hothead.

It was not at all surprising that Henri had found himself in love with a young woman. Being a romantic and considering himself near irresistible, he was either in love or pursuing someone with whom to be in love much of the time. The perplexing aspect regarding Mademoiselle Daphne de Montclair was that she was an aristocrat. While she was not from the upper reaches of society—which would have made a union impossible—Henri was suitable and unsuitable at the same time.

It was clear that his family background, mercantile rather than titled, was less than ideal, but his wealth and rising fame in the financial markets promoted further consideration, particularly by the intended's father. Pre-Revolution arrangements of two such disparate societal strains could have never taken place, but these were new times, and leniencies were afoot. Considerations, they were termed then. In truth, Robert, the constant companion of Henri, was more suitable than Henri for the lady in question, having both title and wealth. But obviously he couldn't be interested in Daphne while his friend was transfixed, and he wouldn't have been otherwise, either.

Unfortunately, Daphne, among her many charms, also had a large dose of feminine wiles, and she was ignorant of how her indiscretions and capriciousness could trigger the insecurity and resulting anger of people in the classes beneath hers.

One afternoon, Robert was walking along the galleries of the Palais-Royal toward the rue de la Paix, where his carriage waited, when he happened upon Daphne. It was raining hard.

"Robert, Robert," she said, rushing through the crowd to his side.

"Daphne," he said, "is Henri with you?"

"No, I was having tea with a friend, and then this rain came up. Is your carriage nearby? Could you take me home, please?"

Who could refuse the plea of a woman who was more like a child? He wondered what in the world she was doing out alone anyway.

He helped her into his carriage and gave instructions for the Place des Vosges, where Daphne's family lived, the same Place des Vosges where his uncle and aunt had lived before the Revolution.

"We never have a chance to talk," she said, turning in the seat to face him directly.

"Are you and Henri going to the theater tonight?"

"You know I'm not in love with Henri," she said in a whisper. Was it to be a secret? Why was she telling him?

"Well, he is certainly in love with you," Robert said, sticking up for his friend.

"I know, and that's what makes this so difficult."

"He will be very unhappy and possibly very angry."

"I know, but I can't give up my chance to be happy to please him."

Robert thought, *But why have you let it go so far?* He grimaced. "Of course not, but if you don't love him and there's no possibility of your loving him, it would be better if you told him as soon as possible."

"I know, and I've tried several times. But I hate to lose the connection with him." She said this as if it were some kind of explanation. But if it was, Robert didn't understand it at all.

"If you don't love him, then why do you want a connection?"

"Because if I lose my connection to him, I lose my connection to you."

This revelation struck him like a thunderbolt, and he searched his mind for any memory of any hint where he might have given her the slightest inference that he was interested in her. He found none.

"But Daphne, that's impossible," he said with some anger given the terrible position she was putting him in.

"But I love you."

"You can't love me. You mustn't love me. I've never given it one thought." He would not spare her his disgust for the insincerity with which she was treating Henri.

He dropped her off at her home, accompanying her to the door. She was dabbing her eyes and obviously crying. The butler who opened the door saw her and looked at Robert with disapproval. Robert could only hope that Daphne would come to her senses before she saw Henri again.

Thinking that Henri and Daphne would be at the theater that evening, Robert decided to go to one of his and Henri's favorite haunts near the Luxembourg Gardens in the sixth arrondissement. Les Bons Temps fronted as a restaurant, but in essence it catered to men who liked to gamble, men who liked to drink, and men who loved women. Madame Estelle Menjou, a woman always too made up, was the proprietress of the four-story *maison* decorated in a fussy style of femininity that explored the margins of excess with lace, silk, and velvet. Red and gold dominated the color scheme of the wall coverings, lighting fixtures, Persian carpets, and upholstery. It was Estelle's idea of Versailles. A classical string quartet played concertos or minuets of either Mozart or Haydn in the grand reception room where everyone gathered, pronouncing the establishment as one where certain rules of decorum were expected. Madame Menjou ran a respectable club that teased with the risqué, naughty enough to be enticing without being illegal.

Normally, Robert and Henri's evenings began with Henri in a gay mood, and while they didn't always start at Daphne's place, as the evening progressed, Henri, Robert, and any other friends who wanted to join them invariably ended up at *chez Estelle*. For Henri, at least the version that came out at night, women and cards were the major attractions. During the day, Henri was all business, concentrating on the bid-and- ask fluctuations of the market. His reputation of charging full steam ahead while others remained timid made him rich and made him dangerous, both to himself and others, including his friends.

Robert, being older and more experienced, tried in vain to subtly and politely restrain Henri's youth and enthusiasm. Robert was often able to distract his friend from his destructive tendencies, but Henri had a stubborn vein, and this quality inopportunely showed itself whenever he had too much to drink. His late nights promoted a propensity for over-imbibing, and his resultant ill temper and belligerence were usually not far behind.

Robert noted that particular evening that it was almost a pleasure to be without his friend to chaperone and protect as he opted for a game of cards. The serious card players played until the early morning, only retiring from the game when the sun rose or they lost their limit, whichever came first. Robert had settled in for just a few hands of pinochle when they all heard the sound of Henri's voice just on the other side of the door.

"Where is that bastard Valmer?"

Alexis squeezed his hand, bringing him back to the present. "Robert, you're in trance."

Discombobulated, he struggled to answer. "I was thinking of Dr. Mendelssohn's idea of hypnosis," he said.

"You were away for several minutes."

"I'm sorry."

"There's no need to be sorry. You may need to see him twice a week."

***

Several sessions with Dr. Mendelssohn didn't have any effect other than to make Robert more unsettled. By day, twice a week, Dr. M was pressing him to remember, and by night, Alexis was probing, however gently, for indications of progress. And Robert was playing a double game with both of them—lying or fending off Dr. M's questions about his past and minimizing to Alexis the impact all this was having on him.

"My darling, you're not talking in your sleep, but you're not sleeping peacefully," she said. "You're fitful, tossing and turning. I can see from the bags under your eyes that you're not sleeping well."

"I feel fine," he said in mock protest.

"Give me your hand for a minute," she said, reaching and taking him by his left wrist.

"Are you going to tell my future or look into my past?"

"A little of both." She said this without even a trace of a smile. He couldn't help being dubious.

She turned his hand over—how could he refuse?—and spread his palm out, gently tracing the lines and indentures in his hand from the tips of his fingers to his wrist. She didn't say anything. She didn't change her expression, which was one of concentrated interest on whatever psychics looked at to see into the future or into the past. Her examination lasted longer than he expected, and he was surprised when she performed the same ritual with his other hand.

When she finished, he asked, "So tell me."

"You have well-defined lines on each hand." She was the picture of seriousness.

"And 'well-defined' means what?"

"I didn't think you were interested in this kind of thing."

"I'm not, but I know you are."

"The two lines that are of real interest in your case are the life line and the fate line. I don't think I've ever seen these lines indicate anyone with a longer life or a life more controlled by fate." She stopped at that, but he could tell that, if encouraged, she had even more information to reveal.

"Only half of that sounds good." He wasn't going to encourage her beyond a certain point.

"Well, you can't complain about the long-life part. And the fate might be good; it's not necessarily bad."

"I feel better already." But in reality, he didn't. Alexis clearly could be dangerous.

"It probably explains why you look so much younger than you are."

He had a hard time not laughing. Could she have said anything more ludicrous?

EIGHT

Robert continued to go to Café Malmaison, though not as regularly as he had in the beginning. Martin had made sure that the entire party knew of Robert's relationship with Alexis, hoping that the force of public opinion would promote a successful conclusion. Success in Martin's mind would see his daughter and Robert married. Robert presumed that if that were to be the case, he might be required to convert to Judaism. But "convert" wasn't quite the right word. Convert meant he was already of some belief and would need to change over to Judaism. "Adopt" was a more apt description. He would need to take up Judaism.

Whenever he did show up for the morning meeting, he was teased about his inconsistency of attendance and the veiled innuendo that he was probably too tired in the morning to get up early. He suffered their little jokes with good humor, but the pressure to do something was mounting. Hadn't it been three or four months, they groused. What was he waiting for? She wouldn't wait forever. She was quite the catch. Did he have something better to do?

Naturally, Martin et al. were thinking marriage. But Robert was thinking more in terms of what was wrong with them living together? They were having a great time together as long as he could ignore his past and she could stop wondering about Henri. And Dr. Mendelssohn had begun to broach the subject as well.

"Have you talked to Alexis about your inability to put your finger on this Henri business?" he asked.

"Yes, she knows all about it."

"Well, not *all* about it," Dr. Mendelssohn said. He paused for a while to see what Robert would say, but Robert couldn't think of anything neutral to say, neutral meaning not too enthusiastic while not obstructionist to his therapy. So far, he believed that he had thwarted any real investigation into his past while not appearing to be uncooperative. Dr. M had placed all the blame on his unwilling and suppressive subconscious; Robert himself was not responsible for the lack of progress. Dr. M decided on another solution, his original track.

"Robert, I think we should try hypnosis."

"Is it dangerous? I mean, could I go into a trance and not be able to get back?" Robert asked.

"I think you've seen too many movies. It's not that you are in a state of robotic response. You can't be made to do something you don't want to. As a matter of fact, you'll be more aware, more focused than ever. And it's this laser-like focus that allows an individual to concentrate and allow his subconscious to come out."

"It just issues forth on its own?"

"No, a therapist can make suggestions and ask questions relevant to your situation."

"Do you think I'm a good candidate for this technique?" Robert tried to look his most earnest.

"Not really, but I think we should give it a try. Your resistance is strong."

"And if this doesn't work?"

"Then we're left with only one option."

"Sodium pentothal?"

"We don't use that anymore. Now I *know* you've seen too many movies." Dr. M. let a little smile gather at each corner of his mouth. Robert wondered if the doctor knew he was being played.

"What's the one option left?"

"Re-creation, reenactment, visiting and immersing oneself in the environment where the past took place. In your case it's inconvenient because it's France. You would need to travel to France and reclaim the past as much as is possible, and perhaps Switzerland as well. Didn't you say you spent part of your early years there?"

"Yes, but everything has changed since I was a child." And Dr. M couldn't know how much. It wasn't just the last twenty or thirty years that Dr. M had in mind; it was more like two hundred years. He would be astonished. Robert closed with "It's very impractical." He knew the doctor would see right through this protest.

"You can afford it. Besides, Alexis would love it. She's a real detective. She's already read up on your ancestry, I'm sure. She would dive right in. She knows how to research things. She's organized. She may think she's a clairvoyant, but she's a hardheaded sleuth." Now he really smiled, knowing how uncomfortable it would be to rest in the crosshairs of Alexis's investigation.

Robert already knew this without having it verified by Dr. M. Robert could imagine how it would be to travel to France with Alexis, particularly on a trip with a mission. Alexis would be suggesting scenes for him, seeing in her mind wee little *Robert* in short pants walking along the Seine on a summer day with his nanny, skimming his boat across the pond in the Tuileries Garden. She would ask endless questions about which house had been his, where he had attended grade school, where his parents were buried. But she would be envisioning an epoch of Paris in the 1970s, while he would be picturing images of Paris in 1750 or thereabouts.

And she would be doing all this in an attempt to help him remember, without realizing the induced pain it would cause him. And for however long they stayed, it would be up to him to put up a good front and, more importantly, keep track of what he had told her. And there was always the risk of blurting out some revealing fact.

He also learned on that same afternoon that it wouldn't be Dr. Mendelssohn who performed the hypnotherapy, but a colleague of his, Dr. Steven Needham. Dr. M reassured him of Dr. Needham's competence and indicated that Alexis also knew him. It all seemed very cozy.

Robert began to feel like he was a gerbil being passed around between doctors busily mulling over the possibilities and their pet theories, wringing their hands about his recalcitrant psyche. "This one's going to take heroic efforts," he imagined them conferencing. Heroic efforts indeed; they didn't know the half of it. He could shut them all up if he wanted to.

Robert had a decision to make, but he could make it only if he could answer a question. And that question was whether he thought he could prevent Alexis from finding out his secret. And if the answer was yes, then could they be happy as a couple with the secret hanging between them? What does one call a question that has no answer? An enigma? And what if she did find out? Would she consider him a freak? In her defense, what else could one call him?

He'd had a similar dilemma before, in Geneva in 1859. Not that anyone had found out the truth, but if he had persisted in that relationship, then it would over time have become clear that he didn't age. He had been living in Geneva for some forty years, where he had fled after almost being arrested in Paris in 1820 as a result of Henri's death. The Paris prefecture of police had issued warrants, and the police had gone to his home in the sixteenth arrondissement searching for him, but he had been warned and had narrowly escaped with his personal effects and had taken a friend's carriage to a small auberge south of the city, hiding there to see if the ruckus would die down. It didn't, because the authorities knew of Robert's previous exile during the Revolution back in 1793. In a way, he was considered to be a two-time offender. The prosecutor was confused because it seemed that it couldn't be the same Robert Valmer, but perhaps his son. If it were the same person, he would have been older, the official reasoned.

In Geneva, which was no longer a part of France after Napoleon's defeat, he was safe. And prudence alone had dictated that he always had kept his fortune in Swiss banks, never trusting other countries to honor their commitments to investors or even the sanctity of their own currency. In his previous exile, he had lived in Zurich, but he couldn't go back there. He hadn't been well known, but he had cultivated a few friends. His reappearance might complicate matters.

And Geneva was preferable, as French was spoken there, so much lighter and sonorous to the ear than German, particularly the German dialect spoken in Zurich. He'd set himself up in the old town, eventually becoming a regular at the Geneva trading bourse and quietly managing his money through currency transactions to the point where he was quite and quietly rich. It was natural that his colleagues often proposed one of their fair-set friends to him, viewed as educated, sophisticated, and single.

And if he had learned one thing, it was that liaisons with women were the most certain predictor of complications being introduced into his life. He could decide whether to get up early or stay in bed, whether he wanted to read a book the whole afternoon or perhaps drink an entire bottle of wine. In essence, if single, he did what he wanted. But the moment there was another person, particularly a female, and because politeness and etiquette required deference to their sensibilities, his freedom of action was diminished. Every decision was like proposing legislation before the Parliament, up for debate, amendment, and revision, not to mention the filibuster. Nevertheless, a relationship with a woman did have distinct advantages that had to be weighed against the other consequences that he knew were part of the bargain.

For example, conversation. If a woman were of a certain milieu, she might very well have ideas that would both challenge and energize otherwise dull afternoons. And there was companionship. Having a companion opened up many social opportunities that were closed to unaccompanied men. And then there was sex and love and tenderness. There was no way to minimize the importance of sex, especially regular sex, with a loving partner; it fostered good health and a positive attitude, and love and tenderness from another person cannot be discounted.

As a result of this negotiation with himself regarding women, from time to time he would take a chance and explore the possibilities that his friends presented. And that was precisely how he had become involved with Jacqueline Le Coultre more than a century later. Friends always meant well, but they didn't have all the facts. He had had to call that off too.

Startled from his reminiscing by a loud honk of a driver's horn in the lane next to his, he jerked his Jaguar back into his lane. Daydreaming was not a safe pastime while driving in L.A. He turned onto Rodeo. He was late. He and Dr. M had explored the hypnosis possibilities longer than anticipated, and now he fully expected to see Alexis's car in his driveway when he arrived at his house. If she had to wait on him too many times, she would begin hinting at having a key. And given her curiosity, would she be able to resist rummaging around once inside alone?

***

As he was putting his keys down in the kitchen and opening the refrigerator, he heard her car coming to a stop in the garage. Soon she was coming through the door. Her professional dress indicated that she was coming from the office. And he had noticed before that hers was not business attire, but rather that she made her selections based on keeping up with her clients' expectations. She knew very well how to be chic in every sense: coif, clothes, shoes, handbag, and jewelry. To look the way that she did, it took money, but that was not a problem for Dr. Roth.

"*Robert*, my darling, your smile is missing. Did you have a bad session?"

"We're not getting anywhere, and now he wants me to try hypnosis."

"And you don't want to?"

"Not really."

"Then don't," she said. "It's not always successful, and sometimes the therapist can make innocent suggestions that can lead you down the wrong path. It's possible that an event can be suggested that the patient will adopt even though the event has never taken place."

"Then I'm not going to do it."

And that was the end of it. He was surprised that she was amenable to a course of action that would signal the end of his therapy, and an end that had not achieved any results. Was he not talking in his sleep anymore? He didn't dare ask.

It wasn't until later in the week that she decided to say something, but it wasn't about therapy or night babble. He marveled at her restraint, but he marveled more at her strategy.

"Do you have any plans for us beyond our current arrangement?"

"Current arrangement? What is the current arrangement?"

"My estimate of the arrangement is that we are lovers, we are companions, we are a lot of things I want."

"But . . ."

"But there's no commitment and no forecast beyond today and perhaps tomorrow."

"Is that so much less than everyone else has, if they're realistic?"

"The best relationships are not based on realistic appraisals but optimism and hope. And without those qualities, the time and emotion invested are constantly measured against an immediate rather than a longer term. Needless to say, sometimes the return on investment doesn't seem worth it."

"If you're unhappy with our current arrangement, as you term it— as it appears you are—then it doesn't matter how I feel about it."

"Of course it matters. It's why I'm broaching the subject. I love you. Can't you tell?"

"And I hope you know that I love you too."

"I wish you weren't so clever. The way you play the game makes it seem that I'm the one that's dissatisfied."

"Then I'll play dumb. Are you saying that you want to get married?" It was the wrong question. He realized too late that he had botched it.

"You're no fun to play with." She pulled one of the barstools up and plopped down.

"Then why would you want to marry me?"

"I couldn't marry you even if you could be serious and ask me." Her eyes were moist. He recognized this remark as a challenge.

"Because I talk in my sleep?"

"No, because I can't figure you out."

NINE

They didn't talk about it anymore that night or any other night for over a week. But Robert knew they were thinking the same thing. And wasn't this the same complaint that had interrupted their romance in the beginning? It was Alexis who had come up with the plan of how they would restart their relationship with the caveat that she wouldn't put too much pressure on him to reveal that which did not naturally come out, and Robert was to try and be more forthcoming. They had agreed to start over and give it a month. Then that month had passed and another month and then another.

But if they were honest with themselves, nothing had really changed. He wasn't demonstrably more open, and she wasn't that good at ignoring his reticence. What had really taken place was a truce, or maybe a standoff. The romance, the idea of being in love, was more important than the issue of the lack of intimacy, or so they thought. What they hadn't anticipated—although they both were plenty smart—was that a relationship is able to progress only so far if the bedrock of trust is absent. Or were they hoping that the road leading to the point where the bridge was out was so long and winding that perhaps they would never reach the precipice?

He said it first. "Houston, we have a problem."

"We do, and I don't have a suggestion for how to solve it," she said.

"I don't want to lose you."

"Nor I you, but over time will the resentment build to where we don't like each other anymore?"

"What do you want to do?"

"I have no idea."

Alexis decided to go back to her place that evening. Robert decided not to object. Perhaps he had already allowed passion to override prudence. When she left, he couldn't quite tell whether she was sad or mad, perhaps a little of each. But he was just as disappointed as she, though he was not confused as to the reason, and that made it all the more difficult.

He had all night and the next day to think it over. She didn't call him; she wasn't going to call him. And he couldn't call her. What would he say? Apologize again? He was the problem, and from her perspective he was the one who needed to either change or at least promise to try. And he just couldn't do that.

A week went by. What was he hoping for? She was more sanguine than he. She didn't seem to want him at any price, knowing what would be required. Time heals all wounds, someone once said. But Robert knew firsthand that time, even lots of time, doesn't cure all ills, just the minor ones, the ones that don't mean so much. The important setbacks remain a lifetime, even two lifetimes, and more.

By then it was Wednesday morning. The weekend would be coming up, and the weekend was the most difficult time. Before, the weekends had been joyful for Robert and Alexis. They searched out special spots to have lunch. They hired a boat and crew and sailed to Catalina. They ran up the coast to the San Ysidro Ranch or the Villa Encantada for romantic interludes. God, he missed her.

He spent the entire day on the telephone with every utility and any other company that provided a service to his home on Rodeo. By check via an L.A. bank, he made a deposit with each, covering a full year's service. Then he arranged with the post office to forward his mail and contracted with his housekeeper to maintain the home in perfect order as if he were living there. He gave her a number she could call if there was an emergency, but he stressed that she was in charge and that he was depending on her to look after things. The next afternoon—and he prayed he would not hear from Alexis—he headed to LAX and boarded an Air France flight to Paris. It was not to be.

TEN

Over the weekend, Alexis drove by Robert's house on her way home from some shopping on Rodeo, but she didn't stop. She just passed by. There was no sign of life, but that wasn't unusual. Robert, if outside, would have been in the back of the house, but the closed garage doors didn't indicate whether his car was there or not. He hadn't called. She didn't want to be egotistical, but she thought by now he would have called.

On Tuesday, she called her father. "Martin, did you see Robert this morning at Malmaison?"

"No. As a matter of fact, we haven't seen him in a couple of weeks. We all thought you two were off in Hawaii or something."

"No. I think we had an argument."

"What do you mean, you think? You either did or you didn't." He sighed. "You two are like a cat and dog."

"I know, and I think that's what we figured out. We can't get along."

"Every time I saw the two of you, you were getting along."

"Oh, we got along fine in every way except one."

"Did it ever occur to you, Alexis, that maybe you're too nosy?"

Oh my God, she thought. *Is that what I've done? I couldn't just enjoy what we had. I wanted more, then more, and finally it was more than he could give.*

She called Robert's cell phone. He didn't answer, and strangely, it wouldn't allow a message to be left. Next, she went over to his house, parking the car in front, walking up to the door, and ringing the bell. There was no answer. When she was back at her condo, she emailed him, saying that she would like to talk. Two minutes after she pressed the Send button, a message appeared in her inbox. The email came back marked "address inactive." The email address had either been discontinued or wasn't accepting mail. Alexis now was in a panic and began to realize that she didn't know one person she could call and ask where Robert might be. Their only mutual acquaintance was her father, and he hadn't seen him in at least two weeks. She did remember that the housekeeper came to Robert's house on Thursdays and Mondays.

On Thursday, Alexis stopped by Robert's house around 9:30 in the morning and rang the bell. After a second ring, Alexis could hear someone coming toward the door.

"Good morning, Dr. Roth," Lilliana, the housekeeper, said. She was in her uniform and had a dust cloth in her hand.

"Hi, Lilliana. Is Mr. Valmer in?" Alexis tried not to look too desperate.

"No. He's away."

"When will he return?" she asked with a slight stammer.

"He didn't say."

"Did he say where he was going?" She thought she knew the answer, and fear began to well up inside her.

"He didn't tell me."

"Do you know when he's coming back?"

"I don't think he's coming back."

"And what makes you think that?" she asked, fighting a growing anxiety.

"He paid me for a year."

Alexis thanked her and made her way back to her car in a rush. Robert was gone. She had scared him away. And he had left without a word. She was furious and at the same time heartbroken. Then she saw Lilliana running out toward her car.

"I forgot. Mr. Valmer gave me a letter for you," she said. "I mailed it yesterday."

Now Alexis was angrier than before. But at least there was a letter. Would he explain? Would he tell her where he had gone and when he would be back?

She didn't have long to wait.

When she returned from her office in the afternoon, the mailman was sorting the mail and placing it in the appropriate boxes. He accommodated her, allowing her to enter the mailroom while he had all the boxes open, only grumbling a little that it wasn't allowed. From the envelope, she recognized Robert's handwriting and the soft-blue fine paper of Cassegrain, the Paris stationer. A reminder of how demanding Robert was about certain things. Indeed, that he was so determined was one of his most desirable qualities, yet frustrating and tedious at times. She waited until she reached her condo, sat down on the couch, and opened the envelope. The note sheet was folded just once. It was barely a page. His writing was large.

> *Dearest Alexis,*
>
> *By the time you read this note, I will have left Los Angeles. I'm very sorry that we were not able to overcome the impediments to our relationship. And please believe me when I say, and I mean it, that the fault is entirely mine. For whatever reason, I can't seem to let anyone get close to me, even someone that I desperately love. We could have continued on as we have in the past, pretending that it didn't matter. But it does matter, and we don't have a resolution. For this reason, I decided that although I suffer a deep sadness, it is better to end our relationship to save*

each of us even more pain in the future. I realize
that my decision might seem callous and selfish,
but after some time, I hope the wisdom of this
solution will be apparent.
    Love,
    Robert

Between sobs, she said out loud, "I don't get a say?"

But it would do no good. It was so final, so unilateral, so selfish. Or was he right? She had two calls to make. The first was to Dr. M. She had his private number.

He answered on the first ring. "Aaron, it's Alexis. Robert's gone."

"What do you mean, gone?"

"He's left L.A. without a word. Well, that's not quite accurate. He sent me a note. Did he seem upset during your last session?"

"No more than normal. What did the note say?"

Alexis read him the note.

"Resistance. You or I or both of us must have been getting close to something. He's running away."

"Then it's my fault. I asked too many questions. I put too much pressure on him."

"Not true. He's generating all the pressure. Are you in love with him?"

"Yes."

"Alexis, don't blame yourself. You couldn't possibly be happy with anyone who wasn't complex."

"I'm not complimented."

"Where did he go?"

"He didn't say. His cell phone doesn't allow a message to be left, and he may have canceled his email address."

"Look, Alexis, you can figure this out all by yourself. Remember, you're a psychologist. Stop playing the victim and put on your thinking cap. He's afraid. And he must really love you."

"Why would you think that?"

"Because he's afraid you won't love him if you find out whatever it is he's hiding. He'd rather abandon you than have you reject him."

That's why she loved Aaron Mendelssohn, the professor, the doctor, and her friend. He had a way of zeroing in on the heart of a problem. And she knew his diagnosis was right. But what could she do about it? She was about to place her second call when she thought better of it and decided to drop by her parents' house instead. She didn't knock at the front door, knowing they would be out back around the pool at this hour of the day. She slid around the side of the house. Their nightly cocktail ritual was in progress on the terrace. Martin hadn't fired up the grill yet, but it was still early. They were probably a couple of drinks away from throwing something on. Martin saw her as she rounded the corner, avoiding the shrubbery.

"Look, Mimi, it's Alexis, our darling daughter," he said. "Must be something serious if she's come over."

"What's wrong, my darling?" Mimi asked.

"It's Robert, isn't it?" Martin said.

"Yes, he's gone." Then she related everything that had transpired. The problems of his reluctance, the discussions, the therapy, the note, and the fact that she didn't know where he was nor how to contact him.

"Good riddance," her father said. "I knew from the first he was a queer bird. You can't trust those French. It's my fault. I should never have introduced you." He was clearly angry. "I wish he were here. He can't treat my daughter this way."

"Do you love him, my dear?" Mimi asked.

"Yes, I'm afraid I do."

"Then you must find him," Mimi said.

"Mimi, don't say that. Don't encourage her to chase after someone who obviously doesn't want to be found," Martin intoned.

"Ordinarily, my dear, I would agree with your father, but I've seen you over the years since your husband's death, and while you've been busy, I haven't before seen the radiance you've displayed since you met Robert," Mimi countered.

"I know. He's made me so happy. He's so different, so intelligent, and so kind . . . until now," Alexis admitted.

"But where would you start? What about your practice, all your patients who need you? It's totally impractical," Martin argued.

"Martin, that's enough! She's got to do what she must. Alexis is smart enough to figure all this out without our help," Mimi finished.

"Thank you both, but I need to go. Robert has a head start, and I've not a moment to lose," Alexis said.

But regardless how smart or how determined she was, she was going to need some help.

ELEVEN

The next morning, Alexis made an appointment with one of the officials at the French consulate on Santa Monica, minutes from her condominium. A Monsieur Tissot listened to her request, which she had crafted to say that she was searching into her distant ancestry in France, and for that research she required the services of someone in Paris who was French but spoke English as well, and who had access to government archives going back to the Revolution, perhaps prior to that. Monsieur Tissot proved to be quite attentive and seemed slightly amused that someone had an inclination to explore beyond what was available on the Internet. He deemed it prudent to counsel, even warn, that hiring a person such as she suggested would be expensive. She indicated without appearing gauche that it was important, and therefore the expense would need to be incurred.

Monsieur Tissot mentioned that it was an unusual request, not at all the kind of demand that was within the norm, such as visas or travel information or even tariff and custom regulations available in their economic section. In essence, he begged for time. He would ask around and see if anyone had a suggestion either for such a person or how to identify someone who might be of assistance. What else could Alexis do but agree?

Driving back to her office, she recalled that the only person she had ever met who had known Robert prior to his appearance in Los Angeles was that man in New York. Now what was his name? She remembered that he was a trader at UBS, but the name . . . Was it Tilson? No. Tillinghast, yes, Tillinghast. Mac, no, Jack Tillinghast. She had it. But would he give her any information? He and Robert seemed to be long-term acquaintances if not friends, and then there was the male protect-the-clan mentality, particularly when it came to women. All she could do was try. And it was highly unlikely that Tillinghast would know how to tip Robert off that she was looking for him.

Tillinghast was easy to locate. He was more than another currency trader. He was an old hand but apparently with nerves of steel. Reports on him indicated that he would bet on a coin landing on its edge if the odds were in his favor. She called him. His gatekeeper, a woman, asked her in what regard she was calling.

"I'm Dr. Alexis Roth, a friend of Robert Valmer," Alexis said.

She was put on hold, and soon he picked up the line. "Dr. Roth. To what do I owe the pleasure? How is Robert? Are you in town?"

"I'm glad you remember me."

"I'm not likely to forget who Robert is with."

"Mr. Tillinghast—"

"Call me Jack," he interrupted.

"Jack. I had thought to tell you another story entirely, but frankly the fact that you remember me, and my belief that honesty can sometimes enlist support otherwise to be denied—I want to tell you the truth. Robert left L.A., left me, without a word. He's disappeared, and I want to find him."

"That wasn't very nice. I hate to bring up an uncomfortable fact, but if Robert doesn't want to be found . . . well, it could be difficult. You did notice that he's a bit standoffish, I suppose?"

"Indeed. That was and is the problem. Do you know where he lived or lives in Europe?" she asked. "That was where you met him, wasn't it?"

"Right. We bumped into each other at various financial conferences, but only the important ones. I was always with an institution, but Robert represented himself. He's a major player, otherwise he wouldn't have been invited. But he was always a little secretive about his whereabouts. It was rumored he lived in Paris at one time, and then someone else thought it was Rome. I heard that his wife died two, almost three years ago in Rome. Come to think of it, I know he had an apartment or a villa in Florence, maybe on the outskirts. And he was always in and out of Switzerland. My guess would be Zurich or Geneva. I'm afraid I'm not much help."

"Oh, but you are." She paused. "I was thinking of engaging a private detective."

He chuckled. "I'd be careful. They'll take your money, and sometimes they'll find who you're looking for and then collect from them too, to *unfind* them, a two-for-none concept."

"You seem to have some experience with this."

"Dr. Roth—may I call you Alexis?—currency people are of all stripes. Extraordinary measures are called for to know the people you're dealing with."

"Yes, please call me Alexis. And would you have a name for a private investigator? Someone you would recommend?"

"Let's see . . . um, yes. There was this guy, French, Parisian, but he must be old by now. I don't remember his name, but I could find out."

Alexis came away from the conversation convinced that honesty was the best policy. Jack had inexplicably gone out of his way to help her. He promised to call back when he had a name.

Monsieur Tissot of the French consulate called while Alexis was in session. He indicated he had a name. She called him back, and he began by introducing all the imponderables in the recommendation. Next, he reiterated several small caveats about how the consulate could not be brought into the situation and that the French government had no responsibility in this enterprise. He also reminded her that their conversation was being recorded. She listened politely, gracefully, and patiently until she wanted to scream, "What's the name?" But bureaucracy has its own pace. He finally got around to it.

"Monsieur Émile Hibou, or rather, Inspector Hibou. He's a former, now retired officer in the DST, or Directorate of Territorial Security, what you might think of as the French FBI. We are not certain that he's still active, but I was able to obtain an address and a telephone number. Do you speak French?"

"Thank you so much. Really, I can't thank you enough. And no, not yet, but *merci*," Alexis said.

Jack called later that evening. "I've got a name, and I remember this guy, a bit of a curmudgeon. Wants everything his way. He must be old now, but maybe he can set you up with someone reliable. He was honest. That I remember. Quite a character."

"Jack. The name."

"Oh, sure. Sorry, I was going on a bit, wasn't I? His name is Émile Hibou. Used to be in the French internal police unit."

Alexis had the name. And with two independent sources providing the same man, he had to be good. But would he do it? How old was he, anyway? A phone call wouldn't do. This had to be in person. She looked at the address. It was in the posh seventh arrondissement. Police pensions in France must be better than she thought.

The telephone rang. It was Tillinghast again.

"One more thing, Alexis. Monsieur Hibou comes from an industrialist family; his grandfather was one of the founders of Renault. He can't be bribed or bought. He must believe in your case. Just a heads-up."

Tillinghast to the rescue. She hoped that Robert and she would one day be able to thank him. But first, she had to pack for an extended stay in Paris, and maybe beyond.

TWELVE

Unbeknownst to Alexis, she took the same Air France flight from LAX to Charles de Gaulle Airport in Paris that Robert had taken earlier in the month. He had a two-week head start. She checked into the George V on one of her favorite streets in Paris, a tree-lined mecca for international clientele looking for the latest fashions. Alexis was not a tourist here, however. With her deceased husband, an art collector, she had visited Paris and the south of France on many occasions during their marriage and even before, when she was a young adult and student. Although she wasn't fluent, she had taken French in school, and after she met Robert, she'd had an incentive to reacquaint herself and improve her French.

She had prepared a letter for Monsieur Hibou, with the help of Monsieur Tissot at the consulate back in Los Angeles, in which she explained that she required his assistance on a matter of some importance, that she was staying at the George V, and that she would meet him at his convenience. She also indicated that Jack Tillinghast of the Union Bank of Switzerland had recommended him.

The concierge at the hotel used the hotel's internal courier service to deliver the letter to Monsieur Hibou's address. The courier was instructed to obtain a signature as proof of delivery. And when the courier returned and provided the signed delivery copy, Alexis was relieved to see that *É. Hibou* was in the appropriate spot.

The next morning, she received a hand-delivered note inviting her to come to an address on the rue de Grenelle in the Seventh at ten the following morning. The note explained that she was expected, and no confirmation was required.

***

She asked her driver to circle the block, because in her effort to be on time, she was awkwardly early. She had carefully dressed for the meeting, knowing full well that not only do first impressions count, but she was an American, and with the French, there was always something to prove in the sophistication department. Chanel should do it. Something modern yet tasteful, feminine but discreet, a Birkin bag from Hermès, a gold cuff from Boucheron, her amethyst earrings from Poiray, and her heels from Yves Saint Laurent. She was immaculate, her hair freshened up in her room that very morning. She was ready for Monsieur Hibou.

(Little did either know, but Robert had an appointment with an attorney just three blocks away from where Alexis was to meet Monsieur Hibou that same morning. If fate had been kind, they would have run into each other. Robert had been in Paris for two weeks, having decided that it was the best place he could think of where he might forget. But he had been wrong. Not only did he imagine Alexis everywhere and what might have been, but he was reminded of all the unpleasant episodes that crowded the past for him there. It was unlikely that they would bump into one another, however, as he was staying at a private *hôtel particulier* in the sixteenth arrondissement. How droll it might have been had the unexpected happened. Though there was little chance, because Robert was leaving Paris the next day.)

The driver turned into a porte cochère off rue de Grenelle and parked in a small courtyard in front of the Baroque building of five stories that housed the Hibou office. The concierge of the building led Alexis to the elevator and selected the fifth-floor button. At the top, there were two sets of highly polished mahogany wooden doors. One was marked simply "É. Hibou," while on the other, a shaded script in gold and black indicated the offices of the Maritime Insurance Company of the North Atlantic.

Alexis hesitated just in front of the doors, collected herself, took a deep breath, and opened the door. This was for all the marbles. She did not have a Plan B. She was surprised to find that a man of around sixty seemed to be the receptionist. He greeted her in perfect English, although with a tinge of accent, and informed her that he would announce her arrival to Monsieur Hibou. Shortly thereafter she was shown into an office just beyond the reception room.

The man seated inside rose in a courtly manner. He, too, was in his early sixties, and extended his hand, but only after she extended hers. He invited her to take a place in the intimate sitting area that was a part of his office. She sat on a sofa that was covered in corduroy velour featuring French blue and cream stripes. He took one of the heavy zebra skin–upholstered armchairs facing the sofa. The office was decorated in the French Eclectic style. Numerous pieces graced the walls—grand etchings of French historical sequences; the French flag, resembling a battle flag, framed above the fireplace; and firearms of all types, mostly antique. A collector's personal museum of found pieces, each one with its own story, Alexis would bet. Finally, it was time to broach the subject for which she had come.

"Thank you for seeing me so promptly," Alexis said, sitting erect and on the edge of her seat. "But I must confess at the outset that, contrary to my letter, I'm not looking for ancestors, I'm looking for my lover."

"Dr. Roth, I've always liked and admired Americans. They get right to the point. No French niceties and diplomatic euphemisms, no circumlocution and obfuscation. No, not at all, just dead on, full steam ahead, *à plein gaz*. And who is he, and where is he?" He leaned back, folding his arms across his chest, not a good sign from Alexis's knowledge of body language.

"His name is Robert Valmer, or maybe Robert de Valmer." Alexis then recounted the entire story, leaving nothing out except the part about his talking in his sleep, thinking she could reveal that later if necessary. Hibou listened and never seemed to blink, and he never made a comment. Alexis was unnerved, because she had never experienced anyone who seemed to listen with their ears and communicate such understanding with their eyes, all without a sound or a nod of the head. He was akin to a father confessor. He seemed to consume all you wanted to tell him without interruption or judgment.

"But I'm not sure you need me," he said once she'd finished. "You have a name. With a name, it's so very much easier. And my job has always been to catch spies or criminals."

"He's broken my heart. Does that count as a crime?" Alexis asked, realizing she needed his compassion, not his pity.

"Yes, Madame, anyone who would break your heart needs to be punished."

"Can you find him so that I can talk to him?" It was a lover's request, but she couldn't help it.

"I really don't do this anymore. I consult with companies about security and personnel. I'm too old to track down someone who doesn't want to be found. But I can recommend someone who is excellent for the job, a protégé of mine."

"That's very disappointing. I was told you're the one who could do this, and maybe the only one. I'm not fond of the *crêpes de sous chef.*"

"This would not be the assistant chef. She's actually better than me, but of course, we can't tell her that." He smiled in a conspiratorial way.

"A woman. I'm not really thinking of a woman for this job." She didn't want to be rude, but she didn't like being put off either.

"You should start. She's a graduate of the London School of Economics, a decorated French combat soldier, and she was an officer in the French internal security services. It's like your CIA."

"Credentials are one thing, but how well do you know her? Have you worked with her?"

"Actually, I know her quite well, and yes, I've worked with her for a long time. I think you two might be *sympathique.*"

"What's her name?"

"Inès Hibou, my daughter."

"Sounds like nepotism." She hoped she wouldn't offend him, but she couldn't quite give up on having him head up the project. If his daughter wanted to help, that was his business.

"It is. I'm glad she keeps me around."

"Shall we work out the financial arrangements?"

"I'll let you and Inès take care of that. The older I get, the less I like to talk about money."

"When can I meet her?"

"I would like to tell her everything you have told me, do a preliminary search, and then she will contact you at the hotel. How long are you staying in Paris?"

"Until you find him."

"Have you decided yet whether you want to love him or kill him?"

***

As Alexis made her way back to the hotel, she couldn't help but be a little disappointed. Hibou had come with the very best recommendation, two even, and now she was relegated to work with his proxy. Just how objective could he be when his surrogate was his daughter? Alexis decided that she wouldn't torment herself with what might have been but would wait and make a judgment after she met . . . what was her name again? Inès Hibou. From the name, Alexis assumed she had never married or was divorced. Not that it mattered. Alexis, having fought through a man's world in the psychology field, knew what it was like. And she tried to imagine how much more difficult it would be in the French army and the French intelligence services. It would be easier to crack Le Cordon Bleu. Inès must be one tough cookie. She liked that, and it helped her talk herself into feeling better.

Normally Alexis would have been out shopping, but she wasn't in the mood. Waiting on Inès to get in touch, plus ruminating over Robert, kept her at once anxious and morose.

Inès called the following afternoon.

"Dr. Roth, this is Inès Hibou. I was wondering if it was too late for us to get together this afternoon?" Alexis said that she would be in the rue de Grenelle office within the hour.

This time, Alexis was led to another office off the reception room at Monsieur Hibou's. And when she entered, she saw a woman she presumed to be Inès, a woman about her age and height, five-foot-seven, with long dark-brown hair in a ponytail, large brown eyes, and a full mouth with the French pouty lips as well as the Gallic nose. She had a beautiful figure, not muscular, as Alexis had expected, but solid. She wore black leggings, a blue-and-white striped sweater, a wide loose belt, and sky-high heels.

After the requisite introductions and niceties, Alexis said as sincerely as possible, "I want to thank you for getting back to me so quickly. And please, call me Alexis."

"Alexis, I know that my father has already explained that this case is what I might call a missing person case. It's not exactly what we get involved in." Her voice was without emotion for Alexis's circumstances. Not a good sign.

"Are you saying that you won't help me?"

"No, I'm saying—actually, we're saying—that this will not be an easy task and that there is a possibility we could be unsuccessful. From what I've heard, you know very little about Monsieur Valmer."

It was the first time that Alexis had heard anyone pronounce Robert's name in French, using Monsieur instead of Mister. It reminded her that she had fallen in love with someone she hardly knew.

"I'm not sure what you are saying," said Alexis.

"I'm saying that it could take some time. It will require traveling to wherever the trail leads, and it will be expensive. And just to clarify, Dr. Roth, uh, Alexis, the majority of the expenses will not be the costs associated with the Hibou firm's time, but rather all the logistics. There will be persons along the way who will have information they will not part with just because they feel sorry for you. These people will want money."

"I understand. When can you start?"

"We've already started. My father left for Orléans and Château Valmer this morning. He'll be back late this evening or tomorrow morning. Your *Robert* has a two-week head start, more or less. We plan to catch up. By the way, do you have a picture of him?"

"No," Alexis said, startling herself, since for the first time, she realized that she didn't have even one photo of Robert. "He was always the one taking the pictures. I'm sure they're still on his phone."

Inès asked for Robert's telephone number and if possible the date or her best guess as to when he had left the United States. She said that unless she or her father called Alexis to tell her otherwise, they would meet every afternoon at three to review their findings until they got up to speed. She also asked if it would be an imposition if, over the course of the next few days, Alexis would make an initial deposit of twenty thousand Euros as a retainer.

Alexis had a good feeling that this sous chef was going to make a mean crêpe.

THIRTEEN

Alexis was prompt. At just before three the next afternoon she was in the elevator headed to the fifth floor to meet the Hibous, father and daughter. Anatole, the receptionist, showed her into Inès's office. She'd learned the man's name after her first visit. He had been with Émile since before the beginning, had even been right at his side in the security service. Monsieur Hibou and Inès were at a small conference table in front of bookcases that lined the walls. Standing hunched over a spread of papers across the table's surface, they invited her to come over and take one of the six chairs.

"I believe that Inès informed you that I made a visit yesterday to a small town just southwest of Orléans in the Loire Valley, where the Château de Valmer once stood," M. Hibou said.

"Once stood?" Alexis asked.

"Yes, you see, it was destroyed by a fire many years ago and was not rebuilt by the owners at the time. But today it is a well-known domain for wine, very excellent wine, I might add—at least the one I had yesterday."

"May I ask, what did you hope to find there?" Alexis asked.

"You indicated that, once upon a time, Monsieur Valmer or his ancestors were de Valmers, and that you had located one Robert de Valmer in some of your Internet searches. I went to the château, or where it once stood, and I also went to the official department offices to see what records there were of the de Valmers. There were actually two families, one of a Robert de Valmer and another a Guillaume de Valmer. The records show that Guillaume de Valmer died by the guillotine during the French Revolution in 1793, and his son, Philippe, died in Paris, the victim of a street fight. There is no trace of Robert de Valmer or his son, except there was a warrant for their arrest that was never served. My guess is they must have fled France, probably to Switzerland."

"I can't see how this is any help," Alexis said.

"Wait," Inès said.

"I was curious what happened to the mother of the young Robert, so I went to the chapel, which is really a private church, that still stands on the château's grounds. And in the small cemetery behind the church I found the grave of Anne Marie de Valmer, wife of Robert and mother of Robert. She was born 1722 and died 1779."

"I still don't see the significance."

"There was a caretaker who took an interest in the fact that I had paused before this grave site. And he told me that last week another man, in his forties, but he could have been younger, stopped at the same grave for quite a while."

"Do you think it was him?" Alexis asked with anticipation. She leaned in toward Monsieur Hibou.

"Who else?" Inès said.

"But why?" Alexis asked, sitting back in her chair with a quizzical look on her face.

"I don't know. Maybe he's looking for something in his past."

"But he never seemed interested in his past."

"I believe that he only told you that, and you believed him."

Why hadn't she thought of that? Alexis wondered. "Could it have been someone else?" she asked.

Inès turned directly toward Alexis and stated quite emphatically, "No. He was there, because two weeks ago he took an Air France flight from Los Angeles to Paris. It was Robert all right. He may be walking the Champs-Élysées as we speak."

"How did you find out about the flight?" Alexis asked.

"That was easy," she said, "and I thought once I knew when he arrived in Paris I would be able to find what hotel he was in, but he must be staying at a friend's apartment or at a private hotel, nothing unusual about that. And property records don't reveal that he owns property here in France. He's not hiding, yet."

"Could he be someone other than who I think he is?" Alexis asked. Her mind raced ahead with the possibilities.

"I had an acquaintance run a trace through Interpol. He's not wanted, never been convicted. Doesn't appear in any criminal database or on any watch list. He's probably who he says he is, but he keeps a low profile."

Alexis nodded. "He's very secretive. What's the next step?"

Inès told Alexis that they would have a team place calls to all the private hotels in Paris, at least the ones that were listed, and ask if they could speak to or leave a message for M. Valmer. It might take a day or two. They were uncertain how many calls would need to be made. Since Alexis had mentioned that Robert's wife, Arianna, had died two to three years ago in Italy, the obituaries in Milan, Florence, and Rome could provide details of any extended family and other information of interest. Perhaps they should not meet tomorrow, but the day after, at three. They needed time to follow up on all the loose ends.

***

Robert had checked out of the *hôtel particulier* where he had been staying since he had arrived two weeks ago from Los Angeles. Having frequented the small private hotel many times when he had come on business in previous years, it provided a familiar environment for him as he tried to get over his loss of Alexis. It was a quiet neighborhood in the sixteenth arrondissement, and one of the reasons Robert liked it so much was the fact that, of all the areas in Paris, these streets seemed to have changed the least.

He wasn't sure of the exact date when it had become a hotel, but it was still a private home in 1816, when he had returned to Paris from exile. He was only able to return because of the amnesty accorded to all those who had been accused of crimes during the Revolution. But for Robert, this period of amnesty didn't last long, as this was when he worked at the Bourse and saw the tragic end to his friendship with Henri in what was proclaimed by the press at the time as *l'affaire Henri*. This precipitated a new escape from France.

Since Arianna's death in 2013, he had not returned to Paris. Arianna, although Italian, a Florentine, had loved Paris the way Robert did. She spoke fluent French and appreciated all the refinements of France. These memories of their visits to Paris moved in on his already downtrodden psyche that was grieving over his latest loss—that of Alexis. He had thought that a Paris stay would lift his spirits and rejuvenate his attitude, but after a few days, rather than rejoicing in the spirit of the City of Light, he found himself on a train to Orléans and there hired a car to visit his mother's grave. It had been a good sixty years since he had been back to the Château de Valmer, the family estate that he had sold after his father's death in 1811. The château itself had burned to the ground in 1948. The current owners, vintners of some renown, had actually enhanced the beautiful gardens, the ones where he had played as a child and remembered so vividly.

His main interest was the *chapelle*, the private church where he had attended Mass every day when he was *fils de seigneur*. He had noisily squirmed in the back pews, where his nanny would whack him on the head to make him sit still. His mother was still alive then. Under her influence, the château was the center of activity for the entire de Valmer family.

When she died, she was buried behind the church in a family cemetery next to her other child, Hélène, who had died as an infant. Robert hadn't known her at all, really. A mother is always special to any child, but Robert's mother and he were inseparable, as she had doted on him as if he were an only child. When she passed, he had felt lost, much as he felt as he stood in front of her grave 237 years later. His thoughts and emotions were interrupted as he noticed a caretaker of the grounds eyeing him, probably wondering why he was pausing so long in front of this one plot.

Back in Paris, Robert took a taxi to the Gare de Lyon and caught the express train to Geneva. He paid cash for his ticket, as was his habit. It was not a strategy born out of secrecy, but rather a habit developed when Robert had received his lessons of life and economics from his father, namely that everyone of any standing paid cash for everything. Credit was not a way of life in the eighteenth century. Given the circumstances, Robert had found it necessary to adapt and readapt to many changes over his lifetime: indoor plumbing, electricity, automobiles, the telephone, not to mention airplanes. The list was endless, but for someone who had to manage both change and the acceptance of new things, it was a constant challenge. He had a few credit cards, all platinum or black, but he used them only in a rare instance where he was not an esteemed client.

Arriving around ten in the evening, he checked into the Hotel des Bergues, a longtime favorite. He was in Geneva to arrange withdrawals from some of his numbered accounts, which would allow him to transfer funds into Italy to a private bank in Rome, where he was certain that the origin of the proceeds would be anonymous.

He had left Los Angeles in such haste that he hadn't fully developed a plan beyond just getting away from the mounting pressure of his relationship with Alexis. He had left with the idea that it was final. There would be no reconsideration. He blamed himself for this circumstance because he had become involved with a woman who was very capable of seeing beyond his facade. Her curiosity and imagination, coupled with her professional and educational background, presented a danger to his secret that he had never before encountered. The modern age of computers and the Internet, not to mention the strides in science and medicine, had made information readily available. What before was esoteric had now become accessible to ordinary folk. And Alexis was not ordinary.

Nevertheless, he was realistic enough to know that he wouldn't be interested in someone who wasn't educated and sophisticated, and in all probability, with this as a given, he would wind up in a similar circumstance with anyone new. Was it possible to live a celibate life free from the close encounters that intimacy fosters? He had never been able to be alone for any length of time. Over his lifetime, women and their roles and status had evolved. But there was a time when women didn't ask too many questions or muse about philosophical ideas where knowledge and logic were required to sustain them. He'd had a lot of adjustments to make, if indeed he had made them.

At the time, it had seemed normal, but if he were honest, he much preferred Alexis to the other women he had known or loved or married. He had never met anyone like her. He missed her. He missed her a lot, but he knew that if he had stayed with her, she would have eventually worked out or stumbled upon the truth. That period was over, he kept reminding himself. It was time to start again. He wouldn't go somewhere new this time. He admitted to himself that he yearned for the familiar.

His contacts at Credit Suisse in Geneva were not pleased that he was poised to withdraw such a large sum from his investment accounts, but naturally they complied, although they showed signs of wringing their hands. For the Swiss, banking is a religion, and these were the parish priests. He was accustomed to their conservative mindset, and their idea of taking a risk was to own anything other than gold or Swiss francs. Wasn't everything else ephemeral? Couldn't it go up or down, mostly down? But they had their place. Robert had learned a long time ago, back in the early 1800s, that rewards came to those willing to take risks. Evaluating and managing those risks was the key.

***

Alexis's fourth visit to the Hibou office on rue de Grenelle was less formal than her previous visits. They were all on a first-name basis, although Alexis could tell that M. Hibou preferred calling her Dr. Roth. To him it seemed more important, more correct. Inès went first.

"We got lucky," she said. "He stayed at a small hotel, Le Tremont on the rue de Lübeck. We're unlucky that he checked out the day before yesterday. The concierge was very reluctant until my father paid him a visit this morning and persuaded him that it was of some urgency that Monsieur Valmer be contacted."

"I had almost given up until I told him it was a matter of the heart," Émile said, building the drama. "I lied a little, telling him my daughter was in love with Monsieur Valmer. It was only a *petit* fib, since you could be my daughter, Dr. Roth. The concierge looked into a ledger that he retrieved from under the counter and found that Robert took a taxi to the Gare de Lyon. Of course, there are many trains leaving this station in Paris for all points south: La Côte d'Azur, Provence, Switzerland, and Italy. He was uncertain as to his destination, but he did reveal, in checking the telephone logs of outgoing calls from Monsieur Valmer's room"—and here the concierge and M. Hibou had danced on the borders of legality—"that his one call had been to a number in Geneva."

Alexis couldn't stand the suspense. "Did you get the number?"

"Yes," Émile said, and he read off a series of numbers. "It's the number of the Hotel des Bergues in Geneva. And I've called the hotel. He checked out this morning. We're a step or two behind Monsieur Valmer."

"Have you spoken to the concierge at the Hotel des Bergues yet?" Alexis asked.

"No, we haven't," said Inès. "And there's not much to hope for. The Swiss are much more discreet and regimented than we French. We won't be able to get a word out of the concierge or management staff."

"Are we at a dead end?" Alexis asked. A wave of disappointment washed over her. They had been so close.

"Hardly," Inès said, "but a curious aspect that we have uncovered about Robert is that he seems to pay for everything in cash. We searched for credit card transactions through multiple databases for Robert Valmer and have found nothing. It doesn't seem to make sense that he's hiding from anyone. He's not wanted by any police organizations, and we presume that he doesn't know that you are looking for him, yet he pays for his two-week hotel stay in cash, buys a train ticket in cash, which keeps him off the passenger manifest, and I'm sure he paid the

Bergues bill in cash as well. Who carries around that kind of cash unless they have banks at their disposal wherever they go?"

"For a person his age, it seems so old-fashioned," Émile said. "I remember my father and grandfather and their insistence on paying cash. They thought credit sinful."

"I think I told you he's a currency trader," Alexis said.

Émile nodded. "And we did find an obituary in *La Repubblica*, Rome's most important and highest-circulation newspaper. It dates from November 22, 2013, and it is only one short paragraph. It gives the name Arianna Soldati Valmer, born 1974, died 2013, survived by Robert Valmer, her husband, and a brother, Armando Soldati of Florence. The internment was in Campo Verano, Rome. Not much to go on, but we did learn that he must have lived in Rome at least from sometime before 2013 until he moved to Los Angeles in 2015. And if he lived in Rome that long, there must be some attachment that he might return to. In addition, there's the wife's brother in Florence. Maybe he can help us understand Robert better. He might even have some ideas where he might be."

"If the brother will talk to us," Alexis said.

"We'll know soon enough," Inès added.

Then the conversation turned back to Geneva. And M. Hibou ventured that while the Swiss were notoriously restrained, some of the staff might not be Swiss and perhaps less rigid. Maybe they could be persuaded to remember something about where M. Valmer had hurried off to just two days after he arrived in Geneva.

"But, of course, that would mean going to Geneva," said Émile. "It can't be handled by phone."

"I'll go," Alexis said with enthusiasm. Anything was better than waiting.

"Of course," he said. "It's a good idea. But I want Inès to go with you. Would you mind?"

She didn't mind. She welcomed the idea of having a professional along. While she knew that she was good at asking questions, she was certain Inès knew a lot more about bribery and persuasion in these situations than she did. And Inès spoke French, as well as several other languages.

Inès immediately proved her point by picking up the telephone and calling the Hotel des Bergues, asking for reservations. She explained that she and her friend, a Dr. Roth, would require two rooms, nice rooms, and one of Dr. Roth's friends, a Robert Valmer, had stayed there only a few days earlier, and that in his conversation with Dr. Roth, he had praised the particular room he was given.

Now, of course, Dr. Roth couldn't remember the room number, but if the hotel could accommodate her, she would be pleased to tell M. Valmer the next time she saw him. The reservation clerk didn't see through the ruse, checked his records, and found that yes, a very nice room indeed, number 528, with a view over the lake as well as the park fronting the hotel. And Madame Hibou would have the room adjacent, number 526, equally as pleasant. Alexis gave Inès the OK sign. M. Hibou had been right. His daughter was clever.

Inès went on to explain that the staff at hotels of this caliber guarded their stations jealously. And the floor maids of both the day shift and the night shift would, in all likelihood, be the same ones who had been on duty when Robert was there. With any luck, they might even remember him.

"By the way, Alexis, is Robert a good tipper?"

Alexis wondered why this mattered, but she knew better than to ask. "Why, yes, he believes in overtipping."

"I'm so glad, because then the staff will surely remember him," Inès said with a small smile of triumph.

FOURTEEN

Inès and Alexis took the same train to Geneva that Robert had taken three days earlier, arriving in the late afternoon, checking into the hotel just in time to change clothes and have dinner at Le Gentilhomme, a renowned restaurant at the nearby Le Richemond.

Inès turned out to be great company and very different from the rigid career woman that Alexis might have expected. Naturally they discussed Robert at some length, and Alexis, given her years of experience with counseling and therapy, knew how important it was for the therapist—or in this case, the detective—to know as much as possible. What seems incidental and unimportant to the patient can be of seminal importance to crack a neurosis, or in this instance, the case. Was this the time to tell him about Robert talking in his sleep? She hoped that M. Hibou would find information that would reveal to her the importance of the mention of Henri. She had a desire to crack the case herself. It might be a secret so horrible that she wouldn't want it known by anyone but herself.

Their conversation jumped around. One minute they were talking about Robert's home in Los Angeles and his extensive collections of various oddities, and then they moved on to trends in fashion and what they might be wearing in the upcoming spring and summer. Under the circumstances, Alexis was certain that she said more than

Inès, and that was a role reversal for her; most of the time, she was the one doing the listening.

Alexis was curious about Inès and her background. M. Hibou had only given her the highlights when legitimizing Inès for this assignment.

"It must have been a difficult decision for you to leave your position in the French intelligence service to join your father," Alexis said.

Inès let a small chuckle escape. "It was never a decision. He is more subtle than that. He asked my opinion when he was investigating an embezzlement case, and predictably, I took the bait. I was partly showing off and partly fishing for his approval. Do we ever outgrow that, in respect to our parents?"

"Not ever," said Alexis. "The only slight improvement is that we begin to recognize that it's part of the relationship, as expected by one side as it is the other. I still act out this charade from time to time with my father, Martin. And he loves it when I do."

"Next, Émile was solicited by one of my supervisors at the agency to work as a contractor on a case of a mole inside the army. He was hired to pose as an arms dealer, seeking small arms and munitions for a sub-Saharan terrorist group. My supervisor thought it would be a good idea if my father had an assistant, preferably a female, since the suspect, a lowlife, fancied himself a ladies' man. The agency volunteered my services, and my father accepted with a knowing smile."

"It must have turned out all right?"

"Wildly. Plus, through a piece of good fortune, the mole was killed in a car accident, but only after he had given up his handler and other sources. All connection to myself and my father died with him."

"Was it after that you made the break?"

"Exactly. And all he said was 'That took long enough.'" She gave a smug look, pointedly imitating her father's demeanor.

"But you appear happy with your decis—your choice."

"Yes, thanks for the distinction."

But when Alexis probed too deep, Inès would give her but a few hints, holding back on any elaboration of her accomplishments. Alexis watched her body language—Alexis was trained in physiognomy and

the signals unconsciously revealed by body posture and movement—
and diagnosed that Inès was simply shy. Whenever Inès spoke of
herself, particularly of some skill that would not ordinarily be the
provenance of a woman, she shifted in her seat, looked down, and
her voice dropped to a whisper. Modesty from such an accomplished
character was an endearing element of her personality. Émile had
probably coached her from childhood not to brag.

But the interest between the two women of similar age but
disparate backgrounds was not all one-way. Inès's questions had veered
from Robert and were more focused on her. In France, fortune-telling,
clairvoyance, and superstition had a long history concentrated in the
communities of gypsies that had always found France hospitable to
their culture, particularly in the south of the country, near Perpignan.

As Alexis related her education and professional pursuits, Inès let
it escape that she had looked at her website, and Alexis was certain
that the curious Inès had read much more. While Alexis's world was
not Inès's world, Inès seemed to respect forces that moved others to
behave in certain ways, even if she didn't understand them or believe
in them. Inès was clearly a keen observer and not one to dismiss any
factor that might contribute to better comprehension of a subject.

"When you were with Robert, did you ever analyze his personality
using your skills as a psychic and psychologist?" Inès asked.

"At first, no. I don't think in those terms when I meet someone,
whether they are to be friends or a romantic interest. And for full
disclosure, there haven't been any romantic interests since my husband's
death until Robert."

"You say 'at first,' but was there a time you began to question his
. . . his . . . what do you call it?"

"I considered it restraint, reticence, then secrecy. I must admit that
I couldn't help myself. I became curious and then suspicious."

"I'm sure this registered with him. Did he change his attitude
toward you?"

"No, we seemed to be on the same team. He even accepted my
proposition to see a psychiatrist. I told him he needed to look at his
dreams."

"Did they make any progress?"

"No."

"And shortly thereafter he left."

"Exactly."

"I think your Robert has a terrible secret that he can't reveal."

"Perhaps, but it must be something that he can't risk someone else knowing. There are all kinds of secrets, believe me. I've seen hard men embarrassed that they stole a small amount of money from a family member when they were children."

They didn't speculate any more about Robert's secret, but Dr. M had alluded to the possibility of a dark memory, just as Inès had. Alexis had tried to fend off thoughts that Robert's subconscious held something so terrible that he couldn't allow it to get out, although now she had to consider it. But a secret is hard to keep, and the more the truth is withheld, the more it seeps out. Freudian slips, inadvertent connections, not to mention talking in one's sleep, can all expose the secretive.

Alexis didn't sleep much that night, constantly searching her memory, trying to connect dots where there weren't any. It was a futile game, and without the participation of Robert himself, would she ever be able to know what precisely had sabotaged their relationship?

**

The next morning after breakfast, around nine thirty, Inès called unexpectedly and asked Alexis to come to her room. *What is this about?* she wondered. They had made no plans, which had left Alexis curious as to how they were to obtain any information about Robert.

Inès was dressed and ready to go out, but standing in the middle of the room was a room-service table with coffee service for two. Alexis knew that Swiss coffee service can be elaborate, and this one included large sterling pots of coffee and hot milk; floral-patterned china with smaller dishes for fresh butter, salt, and pepper; a selection of breads and generous helpings of Swiss fruit jams and marmalade;

and a vase of fresh flowers. Alexis had already had breakfast, but she played along. As they were gossiping, there was a knock at the door.

"*Entrez,*" Inès said. The maid had come to clean the room. The woman apologized for the intrusion and said she would come back later.

"Not at all," Inès said. "We are just finishing up. Please, come in."

Reluctantly, the maid entered. She began her duties in the bedroom. Inès waited a few minutes and then called out to the woman.

"Yes, madam?"

"If you were on duty three days ago, then you must have seen my fiancé, Monsieur Valmer. Reception told me that he stayed in the room next door, my friend Dr. Roth's room," Inès said.

Alexis could see the indecision on the maid's face as her thoughts created lines in her brow. She must have decided there was no harm in answering. "Yes, ma'am, he was a nice gentleman."

"Isn't he? And so handsome, don't you think? But I'm so disappointed, because I came here to surprise him, and now I find that he has left. My surprise is ruined."

"I'm so sorry," said the maid. "He'll be disappointed, too. He was very nice to all of us."

"And what is your name, my dear, so that I can mention it when I see him?" Inès said.

"Giorgina. It's Giorgina," she said.

"And by the way, Giorgina, did Monsieur Valmer say where he was going? Because maybe, just maybe I can still surprise him. He's on business, I think."

"Yes, ma'am. He went to Zurich. The reason I know is that he asked me if I knew Zurich, and when I said no, he said I should go sometime. It was lovely at this time of year, he said."

"It is. Zurich is glorious at this time of year."

FIFTEEN

Three days before, Robert had quit Geneva for Zurich, where he also had accounts, separate and unknown to his bankers in Geneva. It was next on his itinerary. He rented a car and decided to take the route through the Bernese Oberland. It was the long way, the scenic one, to renew his memories of the time when he had first moved to the city with his father. His father knew Switzerland well and loved it, and in the early years of their exile from France, his father had found great contentment spending time in the area southwest of Zurich as well as east in the high Alps of Graubünden. As he became ill and weaker, he had lost interest in everything, including those magnificent vistas that he had once associated with God's majesty.

Robert checked in at the Baur au Lac, Zurich's premier hotel, positioned close to the narrow neck at the point where Lake Zurich outfalls to become the River Limmat. He had a sumptuous dinner in the hotel's dining room and retired early. The next morning, it was a short walk to the main branch of Kredit Graubünden, AG, a private banking concern. He conducted transfers and withdrawals like those he had made in Geneva, and the attitude of the Baer officials was much the same as their compatriots in Geneva.

One of the associates of the chairman, a man Robert knew well, approached and asked if he might have a word. He led him to an office just off the banking floor. It was more like a boardroom, with a large conference table positioned with leather armchairs tucked under the table's surface. The expensive wood paneling that covered the walls of the boardroom was interrupted only by almost life-sized portraits of the founders and early chairmen of the bank, hanging there, watching dutifully over the proceedings. If it were meant to be imposing, it was. The decorations invoked a certain gravitas to the conversation.

Herr Stefan Abendsteig invited Robert to sit down. "Monsieur Valmer, it is so good to see you again. It's been five years or more. We thought you had moved to the United States," he said.

Robert recognized all this as a question rather than a statement of fact. For the time being, he would cooperate.

"Yes, five years. I moved to Los Angeles, but now I'm back."

"My colleague asked me to approve some substantial transfers and other transactions this morning. Of course, there is no problem. Or is there? Have we failed you in some way?"

"No, not at all. I am trying to anticipate my needs. That's all."

"I wouldn't dare ask what those needs are. It's your business alone, but the sums indicate an importance that we haven't seen in some time." He had cleverly asked what was going on without asking directly, knowing it wasn't any of his business.

"Agreed. It might have some importance, but as yet it is impossible to estimate its value, and unfortunately I am sworn to secrecy, otherwise I would gladly reveal the details of my plans."

But rather than satisfying the man's curiosity, just the use of the word "secrecy" was tantamount to waving catnip in front of a cat. While Abendsteig said he understood, he didn't, but he so wanted to, desperately so.

"I understand completely. You know how we Swiss of the banking profession are about secrets. To us they are akin to the Holy Grail, just to reaffirm how safe whatever you would want to tell me would be in the case you require a confidant of sorts," he added, not giving up.

"I am very aware of this prodigious quality, and I will keep it in mind."

Robert finally escaped from the honeyed hands of Herr Abendsteig and realized that he would need to leave Zurich soon, otherwise the higher-ups at the bank would soon be calling him for lunch or dinner to see if they could pry information from him. Robert was known in the banking community as an investor who was in the market only here and there, but in general whenever he committed a hefty sum to a project, it was thought that Robert already had knowledge of the outcome. This myth was not always true, but his investments turned out favorably enough most of the time that his bets—if you wanted to call them that—were accorded the status of a sure thing. The bankers at KG were no doubt trying to get in on the action, and the news of Robert's movements had triggered the human quality associated with greed.

One of his favorite restaurants in the world was Kronenhalle in Zurich. That evening he had the concierge make a reservation, then he walked across the bridge as the river rushed by, turned right at the second street, and entered the beautiful establishment, its walls lined with important art crowded together in a random fashion. Although it had been five years, the staff there recognized him. The restaurant had actually been in operation since 1924, and Robert had gone there often, but not so often that they were able to keep up with the fact that his appearance didn't match the trajectory of his patronage. And there was a large break during the Second World War and afterward, when Robert was more or less trapped in Italy until he had marched over the Alps on foot to escape the Nazis. The staff and owner that Robert had known in the earliest period were all gone.

But this situation of being a regular and being recognized yet not changing in appearance was what Robert had to be constantly mindful of. The Wiener schnitzel, one of their specialties, was as he remembered it, divine, and the red Dôle wine from the Valais region conjured up thoughts that went seriously back in time. Now *there* was a secret for Herr Abendsteig. He was glad he was leaving for Florence the next morning.

Robert had loved Florence even before he fell in love with Arianna. It was a compact city, a medieval city of walls, piazzas, churches, narrow streets as old as time, and art. Art and artisanship of all kinds: sculpture, paintings, pottery, architecture, fashion, and furniture. It had been at a fashion show in the spring of 1997 that Robert had first seen the statuesque Arianna as she walked the runway for Emilio Pucci's line at the Pitti Palace in Florence.

Her family was not pleased with the attention of Robert to their daughter. They had carefully guided her into a position of prominence, the right schools, the right friends, and the right associations. They had in mind that she would be squired off by one of the scions of the old Florentine families connected with vineyards or banking or both. Arianna was pretty and educated, a girl fit for the mannered etiquette of the Florentine life. She wasn't from the *nobilità*, but her family was very respectable. Sure, they could see that Robert was rich and could provide for their daughter in an enviable manner. But there were just two flies in the ointment.

One, Robert was French, not even Italian. True, he spoke Italian very well, but with a slight Roman accent. For Florentines, Tuscans who lived and breathed and spoke the language of Dante Alighieri, only Florentine Italian was sufferable. And the Roman accent was considered almost as hard on the ear as the Milanese accent. Secondly, he had no connection to Florence. He knew no one, and no one seemed to know him. How could he help Arianna meld into the upper social strata if he had no affiliations? And just as important, how could he help other members of the family, namely Armando, Arianna's brother, pursue a career of merit and circumstance?

When Arianna chose Robert and married him in open rebellion of her family's wishes, it created a schism that resulted in a grudge held by Arianna's father until his death and sustained by her brother to the present. Armando had made it impossible for Robert and Arianna to remain in Florence. He spread vicious lies about Robert regarding the origin of his money and why he no longer lived in France. It didn't seem to matter that these stories were untrue, it only counted that the innuendos were exaggerated and effective on each retelling. Florentines stick together.

Soon Arianna couldn't even walk in the streets without being stared at and ridiculed. They moved to Rome, and Arianna never saw her family again except for her mother, whom Arianna met secretly in Orvieto, a hill town south of Florence. By the time Arianna became ill, both her father and mother were deceased. Armando refused to see his sister before she died, and they never reconciled; he even suggested that Robert had somehow been complicit in her death. In reality, she died of cancer. She went quickly.

***

Meanwhile Alexis and Inès were preparing to follow Robert to Zurich and were considering either taking the train or hiring a driver. There wasn't much difference in the time required, around four hours either way. Alexis thought that if they went by car, they could use the time to talk. And after their conversation with Giorgina, it only made sense to get to Zurich without delay. They had missed Robert by a day or two twice already. Perhaps they were closing in, but they had been lucky, too. Alexis didn't need anyone to tell her that, although Inès reminded her several times not to get her hopes up.

The prudent Inès had asked for a chauffeur who didn't speak English at all. That was a tough assignment, since nearly everyone connected to the travel or tourist industry spoke some English, if not a lot, but the car company came up with a driver from the Ukraine, recently immigrated to Switzerland, whose talents included Russian, French, and German, but no English.

"Do you have any ideas about where he might stay?" Alexis asked.

"Yes, one of two or three hotels," said Inès, "and I considered calling them, but I argued with myself that someone might tip him off by casually mentioning that there had been an inquiry. I feel like we're so close, I didn't want to take any chances. Have you thought about what you're going to say to him, if you run into him?"

"I have several options in mind."

"I would discard all but one."

Inès was very wise, and Alexis knew that she would not have had the same relationship with the woman's father had she been working with him. Inès had never mentioned her own private life, whether she was married or had ever been married. Did she have a boyfriend? If so, what did he think of what she did? With her whirlwind career, which some might call dangerous, how did she have the time to meet anyone? Alexis was familiar with the challenges of managing a career and a man. Most men required a lot of attention and reassurance. And a woman had to do this in the face of a man's perceived but sometimes superficial self-confidence. Alexis, and maybe Inès, only wanted a man who didn't need them too much.

And Inès had raised an important point. When Robert left L.A. without a word, definitively, leaving her heartbroken, puzzled, and lonely, she had decided to pursue and find him. She wanted to confront him, ask him why, and debate his reasoning. It had been over two weeks, and the chase had become the quest. If she were honest, the reason she was chasing him was to tell him that she loved him and wanted them to be together. How terrible and humiliating would it be if he gave her a flat refusal? She didn't want to think about it. She wondered if he missed her. Did he think about her? Did he regret hurting her? But Inès was right. Only one of the options had any possibility of achieving the desired outcome.

"You've been away awhile," Inès said.

"Thinking," Alexis said.

"I spoke with my father earlier and brought him up to date on how the Geneva situation turned out. He checked into Arianna's bother in Florence and located an address and a telephone number for Signor Soldati. Of course, we may not need this at all if we find him in Zurich, but it's better to have a fallback position if necessary."

"Did he have anything else?"

"He's still asking around, but it will take some time to find out which city those de Valmers emigrated to when they left France."

"But that's over two hundred years ago. I don't see why it's important."

"It's probably not. But if we knew where they went, it might be a way to trace the family to the present. My father is guessing Switzerland, but he wants to prove it."

Inès took a chance when they checked into the Baur au Lac a little after two in the afternoon. She'd guessed that Robert would either stay in this hotel, the Dolder Grand—although it was a little out of the way—or the Savoy Baur en Ville. As they presented their passports to the reception clerk, she casually mentioned that she thought a friend of hers, Monsieur Robert Valmer, was staying in the hotel, and she would like to invite him to dinner.

"Oh, I'm so sorry, Monsieur Valmer checked out only this morning," the clerk said.

"Yes, what a pity. Perhaps we will catch up with him in Milan," Inès said. Alexis died a little with that comment.

"I don't believe so, Madame Hibou; he mentioned Florence. Yes, he's not going to Milan."

"Well, then, I'll see him in Paris later in the month, but it is a shame."

It would have been too obvious to rush out and grab the next train to Italy. But they would take the first available express the next morning. There was no time to waste. They were gaining on M. Valmer, and he was totally unaware.

This steely French woman mesmerized Alexis. She had no fear, no equivocation or hesitancy in her voice. She gathered information like a sponge, ingratiating herself with people while asking pertinent questions in the most natural and conversational manner. Her victims succumbed slowly, not realizing that they had been manipulated into revealing information that, if they had been asked directly, they would never have revealed.

Alexis could tell that Inès was pleased. But she was stingy in sharing her thoughts, and Alexis guessed that her father had probably taught her to always hold back a little from clients. Don't raise their expectations, he might have advised. Alexis could see how clients might fix on a strategy, a discovery, or a hypothesis, that might not then materialize. Nevertheless, Inès seemed elated to learn that Robert was headed to Florence. It was a much smaller town than Paris, Milan, or Rome. And they had a lead in Florence, Arianna's brother, if he would be cooperative. What might she concoct to persuade him to assist them?

SIXTEEN

The next morning, they caught the 8:25 train, an express, first-class-only train to Florence with two stops, Milan and Bologna, before arriving in Florence in the midafternoon. It gave both Inès and Alexis a lot of time to think and to talk.

"Do you speak Italian?" Alexis asked Inès.

"Yes. Italian is not so difficult if you know French."

Alexis was looking for reassurance: Would Inès be the same help in Italy that she had been in Switzerland? Alexis settled into the trip, retrieving a book from her tote, *A Room with a View*, E. M. Forster's classic tale of an Englishwoman in Florence. She hadn't made much progress; she had read only a few pages.

At one point she checked to see if Inès was sleeping, and when she saw she wasn't, she asked in all candor, "Am I acting like a fool?"

"Who's to judge other than you?" Inès responded without equivocation. She hadn't needed to think to answer, which might indicate its truthfulness.

"But what do you think? You're levelheaded," Alexis said.

"You don't know whether I'm levelheaded or not."

"Aren't you?"

"Not when it comes to matters of the heart. I'm human," Inès said, letting her voice trail off as she turned and looked out the window.

"Thank you, Inès." Alexis knew that there was nothing levelheaded about chasing a man across Europe. But Inès confirmed why she was doing it.

Alexis returned her attention to her book. She had read this classic many years ago and had seen the movie as well. Was she like the Englishwoman in the story? Would she be forced to open her eyes and accept Robert as he was? She was growing uneasy with this pursuit. She knew the signs of obsession all too well.

It wasn't necessary to change trains in Milan. Many passengers, mostly businessmen of the international variety, exited there, given that Zurich and Milan were major industrial and financial centers. But during the twenty-five-minute stop, even more travelers boarded. These were tourists headed to Florence or Rome or the termination point, Naples.

Contrary to perceived opinion, Italian trains were remarkably on time when the railway union workers were not on strike, either on their own account or in sympathy with one of the other unions in Italy. On this day, they were mercifully on time.

Inès voiced the opinion that given the pattern established by Robert of staying in the best hotels, he would be in the Four Seasons, so she and Alexis checked in about a half hour after they arrived in Florence. Inès cautioned Alexis that it was possible, *possible*, she repeated, that they might bump into him. Alexis would need to be the spotter, since Inès didn't even know what he looked like.

Standing in the lobby, Alexis looked around, watching guests entering through the revolving door, others getting off the elevator, and still others coming from the different public rooms adjacent to the grand entry and reception area. Inès casually used the same ploy that she had used in Zurich, wondering aloud to the reception clerk if her friend Robert Valmer was a guest and intimating that she wanted to invite him to dinner.

As they were being escorted to their rooms, Inès had the unfortunate task of informing Alexis that Robert was not in the hotel. There were other hotels in Florence, but none of this stature. She would call a few of them, but she didn't hold out much hope. Inès intimated that without an event of serendipity in which they ran into Robert in the street or a restaurant or a shop, their best bet was the brother. But there was a risk in that, too. He might refuse, or he might tell Robert, and who knew what Robert would do? Would he run?

At dinner that evening, Inès gave Alexis a candid appraisal of the situation. From her tone, it was obvious that she tried to be as objective as possible. While it was true that Robert might be floating around in Florence, the real chance of happening on him was remote without knowing his habits or where he was staying. And how long might he stay? Would he be on the move again in a few days? They had to hope that Armando would help them. Inès had a plan.

***

The next morning, Inès invited Alexis to have breakfast in her room. Like Alexis, she had a lovely terrace under a loggia. Their rooms overlooked the pool some four stories below in the garden. Alexis joined her around nine, and as they were finishing their porridge and fruit and *oeuf à la coque*, Inès went back into the room and made the call.

"Hello, may I speak to Signor Soldati, please?" There was a pause.

"May I tell him what it's about?" the person on the other end of the line asked.

"Yes, it's concerning Robert Valmer."

"This is Signor Soldati. Is he dead?" he asked.

"Who?"

"Robert Valmer. Is he dead? Is that why you're calling?"

"Why, no, I would like to talk to you about Monsieur Valmer," Inès said.

"I'm not interested in talking about him at all. What's this about?"

"I'm afraid I can't tell you over the phone, but it is of some urgency that I and my associate speak with you."

While Armando wasn't interested in talking about Robert, he made no secret that his curiosity demanded he know what and why speaking with him was important. They made an appointment at his office for the next morning at ten.

"What are you going to tell him?" Alexis asked.

"I don't know yet," Inès said. "But we have the appointment. And he is curious without wanting to appear so, which is to our advantage."

"I don't think he likes Robert very much," Alexis said.

"Yes, it is somewhat strange, but many brothers don't like their sister's spouse."

But why wouldn't he like Robert? Alexis asked herself. Her father and the coffee klatch guys liked him. Dr. Mendelssohn liked him, and she loved him. He was handsome, intelligent, kind to everyone, and sophisticated. *It must be something else, and it must be something that happened a long time ago.*

It was a long wait until the next morning. They lounged around the hotel. Although Inès offered, Alexis wasn't in the mood to see the sights or go shopping, not even have a massage. She only had one thing on her mind.

At ten the next morning they arrived at an old palazzo that stood on the north side of the River Arno, just west of the Ponte Vecchio, the old bridge. In this ancient building of Romanesque architecture were the offices of Armando Soldati and his company, a concern that imported Scotch whisky, French champagne, and other wines and liqueurs having exclusive Italian distribution. They were escorted to the second floor, where a suave man of around forty waited for them on the landing. His black hair was combed back, as was the Italian custom, and he wore a suit of a raw linen color with a thin chocolate stripe, a shirt with exaggerated points in an Italian blue, and a tie the color of burnt caramel tied loosely in a big knot, all of it advertising his impeccable taste.

As they entered his office, Alexis appreciated that this man's refinement didn't end with his cravat. Probably everything he was associated with was carefully selected for its aesthetics. He wouldn't like to know that he reminded Alexis of Robert. Inès made the introductions.

"I believe, Madame Hibou, that you said it was important," Armando said, motioning for them to sit down on the leather couch in his office. He took one of the high-backed Tuscan chairs facing them and rang for coffee.

"Indeed, it is. We have an important message that must be delivered personally to Monsieur Valmer."

"Then why not just call him up or go see him?"

"Because we don't know where he is."

"Well, I don't know either. The last time I heard anything about him—and it's been a very pleasant interval, I might add—he had left Rome and moved to the United States. I heard it was Los Angeles."

"Your information is only half right. He did move to America, but then recently, very recently, he came back to Europe, and we have every reason to believe that he is right here in Florence."

Armando visibly winced when informed of this. "It displeases me to hear that."

"Do you have any idea where he might be in Florence?" Inès asked in her most seductive tone, hoping he could be charmed into delivering the requested address.

"If he's in Florence, he could only be in one place," he said rather cavalierly, knowing he had something they wanted.

"And that is?" Inès asked.

"I'm not going to tell you unless you tell me what this is about."

"It's extremely confidential." Inès spoke in an almost lawyer-like manner, indicating confidentiality.

"Then find him yourself." He looked amused by the fact that he was stifling their request.

"The most I can tell you is very little."

"Then tell me, and I will tell you if it's enough."

Nothing is so repulsive as a man being a bully, thought Alexis.

Inès turned to Alexis and told her that she was going to tell him. That it was necessary. She knew that she had promised to keep it a secret, but there was no other way. Alexis looked at her, wondering what on earth she was talking about. What was Inès about to tell him? Then Inès looked at her directly and asked, "OK?"

Alexis paused a moment for the effect, then nodded in agreement and said, "Go ahead." It was hard to tell who was the more eager of the two, Alexis or Armando, to hear what Inès would say next.

"My firm in Paris has been engaged by individuals in the United States, Los Angeles more precisely—Dr. Roth is one—to investigate Robert Valmer, his history, his sources of funds, and his whereabouts. My clients have questions that Monsieur Valmer has left unanswered, and my clients cannot go forward with their actions unless these points of information are explained. A team of our investigators has been tracing Monsieur Valmer's past in some detail, but it will take time. Monsieur Valmer could clarify some of the issues at stake if he were available."

"Madam, you have quite cleverly told me nothing," said Armando, "which I presume was your intent as well as your training. We have a saying in Italian that if you want to catch a big fish, then use the right bait."

"We have a similar truism in French. But I'm not baiting you."

"Does Robert know that you are chasing him?" Armando smiled as he outed them.

"We're not chasing him. I'm not a law enforcement official or an attorney. No legal action is anticipated. Ours is an exercise in greater understanding."

"I'm disappointed. I had hoped he was finally being chased by the police."

"Why do you dislike Monsieur Valmer?" Inès looked straight in his eyes, daring him to tell her.

"I don't dislike him, I hate him."

"Then why do you hate him?"

Armando then asked if Dr. Roth would prefer if he spoke English. He had waited until now to indicate that he spoke English. But he wanted both of them to hear it. He said he had waited the last fifteen years to tell his story to someone who was interested.

He said that he hated Robert Valmer because he turned up in Florence in 1997, and from his point of view had stolen his sister from their family. He had tried to tell Arianna that she would be unhappy with this Frenchman. Armando asked their pardon for his vehemence, but he continued on. And it turned out that Arianna was unhappy. They moved to Rome, away from the family. His father began a grieving that turned into depression, and slowly he receded into a decline ending in his death, a premature death in Armando's estimation. And Arianna's mother—he knew that she had snuck away to Orvieto to meet her daughter from time to time—was never the same. Arianna was the baby, and Robert had robbed Armando's parents of the future that they had envisioned for her, as well as her companionship. The final blow—and here Armando's voice rose—was that Arianna's separation from her family and her inability to conceive children with Robert had, in his own mind at least, precipitated her contraction of cancer and her early death.

A silence enveloped the room at the end of his dissertation. His summary of the lives of Robert and Arianna must have been etched in his mind, as during its presentation he had not stumbled or taken an extra breath. His accusations were well rehearsed. He knew his lines by heart. Finally, Inès spoke—in English.

"Not to be offensive, but young women have often listened to their heart rather than their family. Think of Romeo and Juliet."

"And we see how that turned out."

"Will you help us or not, Signor Soldati?"

"I can save you a lot of time. Do you think I didn't investigate Robert Valmer when I realized he had designs on my sister? We, too, employed agents in Paris and Zurich, Geneva and Rome, and after three months and many thousands of lire, they found nothing except a string of Robert de Valmers, then by the mid-1800s the *de* had been dropped.

"These Valmers were everywhere and nowhere. They were involved in the French Revolution, then banking and speculation in Switzerland, then back in France. Then something happened. We were never really able to substantiate a cause, but a warrant was issued for one Robert Valmer, but it was never served. After that the trail is sketchy. There are indications that some additional years transpired in Switzerland, this time in Geneva, and then by the *Risorgimento*, the unification of Italy, an R. Valmer helped finance the Cavour movement.

"For the next twenty or thirty years, the trail goes stone cold, but stories and rumors surfaced of a Valmer, no first name or initial, who was found to have acted as an attaché without portfolio to the treasury. The next sighting is another story of a Valmer who had a narrow escape from the Fascists and Nazis in Rome during the Second World War. This Valmer is reported to have walked the length of the Italian peninsula from Rome and disappeared over the Alps into Switzerland.

"In the late 1980s, Robert Valmer, the one that I know and the one you seek, appears in Rome. He, too, is a banker and speculator, and very successful at both. He works for no one, has no associates, but is considered a kind of genius. Everyone is suspicious of the fact that he has no background. Finally, apparently because he loves Florence and all it has to offer, he buys a beautiful apartment in the city center. One afternoon he attends a fashion show at the Pitti Palace. My sister is modeling as a favor to a friend of the family, Marchese Emilio Pucci. Robert sees her, and, well, I've told you the rest."

"Then he's at that apartment, isn't he?" Inès said, stating the obvious.

"If he's in Florence, he's there," Armando said with true delight, knowing he was torturing them both.

"Are you going to give us the address?" Inès insisted.

"Are you in love with him, Dr. Roth?" Armando smiled with a knowing look. Could it be that he was jealous of Robert's success with women?

"Is it so obvious?" Alexis said.

"I hope you know him better than I do."

"I don't."

SEVENTEEN

Antonina, Robert's housekeeper in Florence well before he had met Arianna, had prepared the apartment for his arrival. She was proficient in all aspects of managing a household: cleaning, ironing, cooking, stocking the home with supplies, and forwarding mail and messages. But her most outstanding quality, and the one for which Robert kept her permanently employed even when he was not in residence in Florence, was her discretion. She might as well have been deaf and dumb when it came to any details about Robert Valmer.

Unmarried and without children, her family in distant Naples, she lived alone and minded her own business; she was not a gossiping type. Robert had carefully screened her when she was first retained, gradually according her more responsibility and more compensation. Antonina had quickly understood the relationship between her prudence and her future. Over the course of years, Robert had learned that he could entrust her with his comings and goings. He guessed that she considered him rich, private, and eccentric. And her opinion, while not important in the overall scheme, served Robert well. She never mentioned his unchanging appearance.

His apartment was located on the Via Romana, its name indicating that once upon a time this street had served as the main road from Florence to Rome. It entered the city center from the south through the gates of Porta Romana less than a mile from the Arno River. Robert's apartment was about halfway between the entry gates and the river. The eight-room space was once a convent in the sixteenth century that cloistered an order of Catholic nuns. As a result, every room had its own domed ceiling with frescoes depicting various Biblical stories, particularly those of Christ and his interaction with women: Mary, his mother; Mary Magdalene; the Samaritan woman at the well; and others. The colors had faded, but the hues of blue and ochre, terra-cotta and green were still visible, even enhanced by their antiquity.

Robert had bought the apartment as a getaway from Rome a year or two before he had met Arianna. Rome was a busy city full of bustle and aggressiveness. Florence was subtle, more refined, plus Robert didn't like staying in one place too long. When he did stay too long, then invariably his associations would build until there were too many questions for which he could not provide answers. More than once a friendship or relationship had needed to be sacrificed because the other person's desire to know remained unfulfilled. And he didn't need to go back too far in time for an example of that. What more could he say about the Alexis relationship other than that it had been spoiled by his inability to provide information about himself that Alexis deemed important?

Antonina was not at Via Romana when he arrived. She knew that he liked to settle in alone, and he had given her the rest of the week off, wanting to adjust to being back in Florence without her underfoot. She had stocked the refrigerator and the pantry with the necessities as well as his favorites: bread, cheese, Italian sausages, and wine.

After unpacking his bags, Robert took a shower, put on some white tennis shorts, a white polo shirt, and some blue espadrilles, poured himself a glass of white Orvieto wine, opened the French double doors of his bedroom, and wandered out onto the terrace and into the garden. An early spring snap had brought out the geraniums, azaleas, and the bougainvillea. Antonina must have supervised the gardener's raking of the pea-gravel walkways traversing the formal Florentine layout, as all the strokes were brushed in a pleasing pattern.

Sitting on one of the stone benches at the back part of the garden, he looked out over the Boboli Gardens, the largest public space in Florence. In the late afternoon, the tourists had disappeared, drifting back to their hotels and pensions, preparing for dinner and other evening pursuits. What remained was a perfect stillness, a serenity imposed by nature.

Finally, Robert breathed slowly. He had come to rest. Since leaving Los Angeles, he had hardly stopped. This constant movement had been vaguely therapeutic because the distraction of activity helped avoid the pitfall of thinking. But now that Robert was still, thoughts began to enter his mind in a slow roll. Like the tide coming in, each wave capturing more of the shore, thoughts of Alexis and what might have been rose higher and higher in his thoughts. And then the inevitable questions arose. Had he done the right thing? What if he had just told her? Wasn't it unbelievable? Well, it was too late to second-guess himself. There's little respect for deserters, and that is what he'd done to Alexis, desert her. She was undoubtedly angry. As she had every right to be. And it was for that reason that he had left without a word. He wanted her to forget him, and he had reasoned that anger would do the trick. He wished he had his own strong emotion that would similarly erase his love for her, but he knew from the short time of their separation that it was going to be a long pull. *Well, for damn sure,* he told himself, *thinking constantly about it would not help. Put it behind you,* he kept saying to himself.

He went inside. Maybe coming to Florence was a mistake.

***

As he walked down to the river the next morning and across the Ponte Vecchio, arriving at the Piazza Santa Trinità, he found himself recalling scenes of Arianna, having cappuccinos with her at the café bordering the piazza, or shopping for scents at Santa Maria Novella, or splurging at the *gelateria* on ice cream with pistachio, or an early-afternoon film in the galleries off the Piazza della Repubblica. He had left Rome because he couldn't dislodge the loss of his wife from his memory. He had run away to Los Angeles, which hadn't solved the problem. He had only created a new one.

He asked himself if he had made a mistake in allowing the relationship with Alexis to go too far. While planning his move to America, he remembered, he had promised himself to refrain from making close friends and avoid situations that could put him in the limelight. He felt weak to have given in so easily to his desires. But he hadn't anticipated Alexis. She was different. And he loved that difference. Why couldn't they have cherished their relationship more than they did? He had to stop thinking about it. It was too late to do anything about it, and besides, the real culprit was his intransigence about his secret.

***

Robert knew after a day or two that Florence wasn't the answer. Nevertheless, he loved its beauty, for it was like an open-air museum. Florentines didn't need to study art in school, as it oozed from the very streets they walked and was registered by osmosis in their character. He wondered if he should put the apartment up for sale. It would sell quickly at a high price because of its uniqueness. But it would be a difficult parting. He had, over a period of years, perfected its decoration with objects that he treasured while modernizing all the internal systems, never marring the historical significance of its interiors or architecture.

At one time, he had looked forward to bringing Alexis there. He had no financial pressure that prompted him to sell, and future appreciation of the house would more than cover any continuing expenses of maintenance, taxes, and Antonina. If he could arrive at a new plan and execute it, he could revisit the decision on whether to sell the Florence apartment or not.

Every evening in Florence, he watched twilight come while sitting in the garden, staring out over the expanse of the Boboli Gardens, usually with a white wine of the region. As much as he thought about what to do with his life from this point on, he spent more time thinking about what he had given up. When he left Los Angeles and Alexis, he had anticipated the sorrow and the sleepless nights that failed love affairs generally provoke. He held out the promise that time would lessen the pain, but it had been almost four weeks, and his initial euphoria of being away from the pressure of the questions and suspicion had now turned to doubt. He had made a mistake. He knew it.

He missed her.

EIGHTEEN

Signor Soldati refused to give Inès and Alexis an answer on whether or not he would tell them the location of Robert Valmer's apartment in Florence. He had taken ten minutes to beg for more time, and when pressed, he proposed several days to think about it. Inès argued that it was too long, suggesting that the only thing a delay would accomplish was that Robert might decide to leave the city for another destination. Over the past three weeks he had exhibited an inability to stay put.

But Soldati wouldn't budge, and Alexis pleaded silently with Inès not to press him any further, worried that he would become angry and refuse to help them at all. Alexis was accustomed to people requesting more time. In her practice, patients who requested more time, with the excuse that it was a difficult decision and they needed to consider all the factors ad nauseam, were really just procrastinators. But in Soldati's case, he had made her and Inès aware of his distaste for Robert, so it was difficult to understand why he would want to thwart them from finding him. Unless he wanted to deprive Robert of any chance of happiness with her.

When they were back in the car, Alexis broached the subject of Soldati's refusal with Inès. She advanced the happiness theory, but Inès had a different hypothesis. She suggested that he wanted to see if he could use their interest in some way to get even with Robert. She supposed that he did need some time to try and figure out some angle to antagonize, at the least, or better yet, sabotage Robert's prospects. Alexis didn't mention it, but she just prayed that Soldati wouldn't call Robert. But why would he?

Arriving back at the hotel, they stopped by the concierge's desk to pick up their keys and any messages. They didn't expect any, but there was one. It was a telephone message that read: "Arriving tomorrow morning in Florence, taking evening sleeper. Émile."

"Would he come to Florence if he didn't have something important?" Alexis asked.

"No. It's puzzling."

Inès and Alexis agreed to have breakfast together on the terrace off the dining room of the hotel the next morning. In checking with the concierge, they found out the overnight train from Paris would arrive—if on time—at 7:45. They figured Émile would be at the hotel an hour later. They met at nine in the dining room, but Émile hadn't yet appeared.

Alexis hadn't slept much the night before, worrying about what could prompt an overnight train trip to Florence. Wouldn't a simple telephone call to Inès do? Why not an email or text message? Maybe Émile wasn't as adept at the tech world as he was at investigation.

They were finishing breakfast—just fruit, yogurt, and a bread basket—when Inès said, "There he is."

He was coming toward them. He looked perturbed, his face drawn in a frown, his briefcase strap hiking up his suit, which was wrinkled beyond redemption. He greeted Alexis and gave Inès the French air kiss on each cheek. He quickly took a seat at their table, and when the waiter asked, he ordered coffee.

"Émile, what is it?" Inès asked. "It must be important. Why didn't you call?"

"Excuse us, Alexis," he said, "but could you allow Inès and myself some privacy for a few minutes? I need to discuss something with her."

Alexis could hardly say no, but after all, she said to herself in a bit of pique, she was the one paying for all this. She almost said something, but then thought better of it. She could always demand to know if they didn't tell her soon after their little conference. She went inside the lobby of the hotel, but through the generous floor-to-ceiling French doors all along the terrace, she could still see them talking. More important, she saw Émile talking and Inès reacting.

She wasn't sure that they were unaware she was watching, so she moved to an angle where she was invisible to them. Then she saw Émile take out something—it looked like a single page—and give it to Inès. She looked at it intently for more than enough time to see it. No, she was not just looking at it, she was studying whatever it was.

For God's sakes, what could it be? Had Robert been in jail at some point? Was he guilty of some crime? Had he come to the United States to avoid whatever it was? A thousand premonitions ran rampant through her mind. But the most important thought was: Had she fallen in love with a liar?

Inès and Émile continued their parlay for a good thirty minutes. They never looked up or looked around to see where she was. This was intolerable. She marched right out to the table and said, "You've had long enough. What's going on?"

"Of course, please sit down. My father has something to show you."

But Émile didn't show her anything; instead he began to explain what he had been doing while they had been tracking Robert. He had contacted people that he had known well once upon a time and could count on, but he found that now they were more reluctant. Most of these sources worked in the government bureaucracy in Paris or one of the departments, the administrative divisions of France similar to the states in the U.S.

The reason he had to get in touch with these functionaries was because, with such a lack of information on Robert Valmer, it had been necessary to search within the state archives to find such facts as dates of birth, any marriages, divorces, children, etc., and any other pertinent details such as property records, taxes, companies owned, or other proprietorships, and even any convictions for felonies. Surely Monsieur Valmer, with a family tracing its roots back to the French Revolution and before, would generate a copious amount of documents confirming the activities of his family as well as of himself. When his contacts turned up nothing, Émile was surprised and even thought that perhaps his informants in the various government record offices were being reticent or lazy. But each one assured him that there was either nothing or so very little of Robert Valmer that it was altogether quite puzzling.

"Monsieur Hibou, please get to the point," Alexis said. She was out of patience.

"All right. I apologize in advance for the paucity of information and the uncertainty as to what it all means. We know enough to be suspicious, but not enough to understand."

"Tell me what you have."

"We know that the original de Valmers indeed lived in the Château de Valmer just southwest of Orléans. There was the father, Robert, and the son, also Robert, you would say Junior. He was born circa 1750, but maybe earlier. Madame de Valmer, Robert's mother, died before the French Revolution, and there was an infant daughter who didn't survive childhood. They are buried behind the Chapelle de Valmer. We also know that it was probably your Robert who visited these graves a few weeks ago. Why? We don't know. But it is not uncommon for individuals with a long lineage to visit where it all started."

He continued. "Then when the Revolution broke out in 1789, the de Valmers found themselves on the wrong side. There was an incident in Paris where a cousin, Philippe, was killed by a mob, and Robert was with him but escaped. Robert's uncle was guillotined only a few weeks after Philippe died. The two Robert de Valmers, father and son, escaped and traversed France. We don't know how, but they crossed the border into Switzerland at Basel. There were warrants issued for their arrests in France. They turned up a year later in Zurich. The father never returned to France. He died in Zurich and was buried in a small village, Davos, in the Swiss Alps. Then Robert, the son, melts into nowhere."

"But all this is ancient history," Alexis said somewhat impatiently, putting her coffee cup down with a flourish.

"It is, but this part is the period where we know the most. As the story progresses, there are fewer facts, and those facts are not as reliable as the ones which I've just recited."

"But you and Inès talked for thirty minutes. Surely there must be more." Her plea was founded on suspicion that they were keeping something from her. Her face was flushed.

"You're right, be patient with me. I'm trying to be clear, and it isn't easy."

"I'm sorry. Please go ahead."

"OK, we don't know where Robert went, but in 1816, after Napoleon's second defeat and ultimate exile to St. Helena, a Robert Valmer, no longer with the *de* in his name, shows up in a few property, banking, and tax records in Paris. It appears from those documents that he was exceedingly rich and was involved in the Paris Bourse as a trader and investment banker. There is no evidence that he was married. The next entry we find in any official record is, believe it or not, another warrant for the arrest of Robert Valmer. The reason this warrant was issued was for the offense of dueling. At the time of the Bourbon Restoration, this was a practice that was outlawed. Unfortunately, the circumstances of the duel were not available, although there may be other sources for this information. We're still checking. Nevertheless, we must assume that someone was killed in this duel, and we know that it wasn't Robert. This Robert, as the Roberts before him, also escaped, but this time to Italy."

"What about present-day Robert? Any news on him?" Alexis asked, checking her nails in a sarcastic fashion.

"That depends."

"On what?"

"On this," he said, handing her that same sheet of paper she had seen earlier when he passed it to Inès. Now she saw it wasn't a piece of paper but a photograph, an eight-by-ten black and white. She looked at it carefully; it was a photograph of Robert. It showed him at a sidewalk café, and from the look of it, it appeared to be Paris. There was a young woman sitting with him, a very beautiful woman; a bottle of champagne and two glasses were on the table. They didn't realize they were being photographed, for they were smiling and in the middle of drawing close to each other as if for an embrace. A caption under the photo said, "Robert Valmer with the Italian actress Mina dei Fiori in St. Germain enjoying the spring weather." Émile explained that it was the only photo that they had found of any Robert Valmer.

"Is that your Robert?" Émile asked.

"Yes, that's Robert." Alexis blinked and then refocused on what was before her.

"Is it a good *likeness* of him? Because remember, you didn't have a photo of him." Émile asked this in a halting manner, as if he was almost fearful of the answer.

"No, that's definitely him, although he's always so in fashion. He looks a little different. He's always so debonair. Is this woman famous?" Alexis shifted nervously in her chair as she was asking the perennial female question: Is there someone else?

"I don't think you need to worry about it."

"And why not?"

"I had the same impression as you. There was something not quite right about the photograph. Of course, until now, I couldn't be absolutely certain that it was Robert, your Robert. Back in Paris, I studied the photo over and over, but then I took out my loupe to see if either of them had a wedding ring on. They didn't, but then it became really curious, to say the least."

"Why?" Alexis asked.

"How old did you say Robert was?"

"He told my father he was forty-eight, but everyone thinks he looks younger."

"Exactly. So as I was scanning across the photo"—he pointed to a part of the photograph—"there, lying on their table I see a newspaper, *Le Monde*. It's folded, but I can plainly read a portion of the headline for that day, 'Alain Juppé, Grève.'"

"I'm sorry, who is Alain . . . ?" Alexis asked.

Inès finally said something. "Alain Juppé was the prime minister of France during the strikes in 1995."

It took what seemed like a long time, but it was really only seconds before Alexis could grasp the significance of the telling facts in the photograph. In the first place, from Robert's appearance, it was as if the photograph had been taken in the last few weeks, but the clothing of the two characters didn't match the current trends. Alexis didn't know from exactly which period the fashions came, but it was earlier. Then the telltale newspaper lying on the table—Robert must have been reading it while waiting for the young woman and had put it aside when she showed up—reported a story that could only have been relevant within the particular space of a few days. And that time frame was in 1995. So far Alexis hadn't said anything, but Inès and Émile were leaning forward, looking for her reaction, literally balanced on the edge of their seats.

"Robert lied to me about his age," Alexis said.

Neither Inès nor Émile laughed when she said this. In truth, they all were searching for a plausible explanation, but they were all searching for the answer within their own realms of experience. They weren't thinking beyond what they already knew. Their parallel thinking centered on what could be termed a roundup of obvious explanations. It's true that some older men can look younger than they are—testosterone injections, rigorous physical training, powerlifting, Botox, hormone injections, spa treatments, massage, and even plastic surgery can preserve or extend the youthful appearance, provided that the outside shell, the skin, is elastic enough. But the photo didn't lie.

Inès and Émile had only Alexis's word that the man in the photo was Robert. They hadn't seen any other picture of him. And it seemed to both of them that this man in the photo looked to be in his late thirties or early forties. What they couldn't appreciate was that the man in the photo was in fact the Robert Valmer Alexis had last seen less than a month ago. But Alexis busily calculated that even if Robert were only thirty-five in the photo, more than twenty years had passed since 1995. Inès and Émile had already made this calculation before Alexis had rejoined them on the terrace, but they began with Robert's stated age of forty-eight plus twenty years, which would make him a man of sixty-eight, definitely a senior. This was what all the discussion had been about. Now she understood why Émile had not called or emailed them. How could you explain it over the phone?

How could you explain it at all?

NINETEEN

Armando observed that it had been three days since the French woman
and the American doctor had visited him seeking the whereabouts
of Robert, and he couldn't depend on their patience to last forever.
In fact, he had thought that they would have called by now. He had
guessed correctly that the American woman, Dr. Alexis Roth, was in
love with Robert Valmer, and although they must have had a falling-
out of some kind, she had obviously followed him to Europe in the
hope of reconciling. Now all Armando had to decide was whether
or not to tell them where Robert's apartment was in Florence. But to
do this, he had to imagine which option would be the most likely to
deliver unhappiness to the man he despised the most.

It was possible that Robert didn't love this woman, and if she
showed up on his doorstep, he could make fast work of telling her
arriverderci. But there was the chance that they could reconcile and
live happily ever after. Just thinking that, by some stretch, Robert
might be happy made the decision easy. Armando would warn Robert
that there was an American woman in Florence looking for him.

Armando had his chauffeur deliver an envelope to Robert's address
that very afternoon. The note inside simply stated that it had come to
the attention of the sender, who preferred to remain anonymous, that
an American woman along with a French woman, possibly a private

investigator, were looking for Robert Valmer. The chauffeur had been instructed to watch the apartment after delivering the envelope, to determine what Signor Valmer would do after he had had time to read the note. If it seemed he was leaving the city, then the chauffeur was to deliver another envelope to the Four Seasons Hotel to Madame Hibou.

And as Armando had anticipated, the chauffeur, stationed strategically, saw Robert returning to the apartment and presumed that he would collect his mail from the box located in the courtyard. What the chauffeur couldn't see was that the housekeeper, Antonina, had left the note on a round marble table just inside the foyer behind the two red-painted doors. Robert would surely recognize the elegant stationery of Pineider, the Florentine paper merchant, and perhaps waste no time opening it. Armando knew it would come as a shock to Robert that it was known he was in town, and Armando was certain that, although the note was anonymous, he would narrow the field of potential senders to two or three, Armando being one. As later reported by the chauffeur, judging from the time lapse between when Robert had entered the apartment and when the chauffeur saw him descend the steps with his luggage, place it in the Lancia parked nearby, and leave, there was little doubt that the note had precipitated an abrupt departure. The chauffeur's next mission was to deliver the envelope with Robert's address to Inès and Alexis's hotel.

If Armando knew his man, then Robert would, after some thought, realize who had been the person to warn him. He would wonder why. He was sure that Robert didn't expect any favors from him, although perhaps he might imagine incorrectly that time had softened some of the feelings. He would never know the level of animosity he harbored. Meanwhile Inès and Alexis waited.

***

"It's been three days. I think we should call or just go back to Armando's office," Alexis said.

"Well, we can't call, because he can just refuse to help us and hang up. Then what will we do? And we can't go to his office without an appointment. These Florentines are sticklers for etiquette and good form. But tomorrow, I agree, we'll have to do something," Inès said.

But it wasn't necessary after all, because the next morning Inès found that someone had slipped an envelope under her door. She quickly opened it and read the one-line message: "39 Via Romana."

My God, she thought, *he's near the center of town. We could have run into him at almost any moment.* She immediately called Alexis.

"I've got it. Robert's address. Armando must have sent it over last night," Inès said.

"Where is it? Can I go over now?" Alexis said.

"Yes. Do you want me to go with you in case?"

"In case of what?"

"I don't know."

Within the hour they were in a taxi headed over the Arno to Via Romana. In less than fifteen minutes, they had paid the fare and were standing in front of a small courtyard. In the corner there was a small green door with the number "39" over it, hand-painted on two ceramic tiles, a button for a doorbell, and a letter box. Inès rang the bell. They waited. They rang again. More minutes passed, and finally a woman's voice came from a distance. "Who is it?" she said in Italian.

Inès responded, saying, "Friends of Signor Valmer."

"Signor Valmer is not here."

"When will he be back?"

"I don't know."

"Did he go into town?"

"No, he left last evening. He's not coming back for some time."

Robert had given her the exact words to say at the appropriate moment, no more, no less. Inès reluctantly offered the translation of what had been said. A tear welled up in the corner of Alexis's eye, but she recovered her composure almost immediately and asked Inès if there were any way to trace him.

They walked down the Via Romana toward the Ponte Vecchio, and when they had reached the other side of the bridge, they hailed a taxi to return to the hotel. Inès had already called Émile and given him the bad news. Robert had escaped again.

Although Inès had spoken in French to Émile, Alexis understood enough of their discussion regarding the futility of chasing someone who didn't want to be caught. What was next? What should she do? What could she do, now that Robert knew that she was in Europe looking for him? He would be doubly difficult to find. He would need to be lured out.

"Do you think it was just bad luck that we missed him?" Alexis asked.

"No, I think Armando warned him," Inès said.

"But why?"

"To spike any chance of his happiness. He warned him first, and I guess as soon as he was sure he'd left, he sent the note to us, probably to keep us from contacting him again. His vendetta is against Robert. You just happen to be an innocent bystander," Inès said.

Alexis said that they could talk about it later. She needed time to think, knowing that Inès and Émile would understand that she might be considering giving up. When she reached her room, her cell phone buzzed, indicating some kind of message. She received numerous text messages and emails per day, as well as telephone calls from her clients inquiring when she would be returning to L.A. Alexis had been able to satisfy most of them by holding sessions on the phone. Naturally she picked up the extra charges for this unusual, but in this case necessary, arrangement. But when she looked down at her phone, it wasn't a text message; it was an email, and she was stunned to see that it began with "My dearest Alexis." She opened it quickly and saw that it was indeed from Robert. His email address had been reactivated. She hadn't tried it in several weeks.

She sat down on the couch and read.

> *My dearest Alexis,*
>
> *Please let me persuade you that our relationship cannot enjoy what both of us would want, rather it would gradually deteriorate due to my inability to share with*

you the most intimate details of my life. Although we have tried to minimize this shortfall, it always hums in the background. For this reason, I believe that it is best that you forget me. While I love you, I love you too much to know that, day by day, I would be unable to fulfill your dreams.

Robert

Alexis wrote back immediately.

Can't we at least talk? You have my number. I'm at the Four Seasons here in Florence. Please call me.

She knew he wouldn't respond. And she knew why he wouldn't respond, and it wasn't because he didn't love her, it was because he loved her too much, as he'd said. She called Inès to tell her of the email, although there was a side of her that was embarrassed.

In the afternoon, Alexis joined the Hibous in the lobby. She knew they must be wondering what steps she wanted to take, given the recent developments. Maybe they even had a few ideas of their own.

Émile went first. "We have received some new information regarding Robert this afternoon by DHL from one of our sources in Paris. We have learned that the warrant that was issued for Robert Valmer in 1820 was for dueling; he killed a friend, one Henri Clement. The details are still incomplete." Émile looked to Alexis for a reaction.

Alexis suppressed a gasp. This had to be the Henri of the dream. What other explanation was there? But why would Robert, her Robert, be so intense about it?

"But do we know where he went?" Alexis asked.

They didn't, but perhaps they could find out.

Alexis knew what she wanted to do. "As improbable as it sounds and as ill-advised as it may seem, I have decided to continue the search for Robert and find additional details about his life prior to coming to the United States. I hope that you can agree with, if not bless, my decision and that you will continue to help me."

"As I told you in the car on the way to Zurich," Inès said, "we French are the last ones to preach practicality."

"Did he say anything about how you found him?" Inès asked.

"No, there was no mention of that," Alexis said.

"But Alexis, my dear, how will you manage to change his mind? He seems so resolute," Inès said sympathetically.

"I have a plan," she said with a distinct glint in her eye.

And then Alexis moved closer to both of them and spoke in hushed tones, and from time to time she looked over her shoulder and around to see if there were any potential meddlers nearby. It didn't take more than a few minutes for her to explain her strategy, although she left out her considerable psychic and psychological powers to persuade people to reveal themselves.

"It's brilliant," Émile said.

"Robert Valmer is a lucky man," Inès said.

TWENTY

The next morning the three of them were on the train for Paris. They could have taken a plane from Pisa, but they would have had to travel to Pisa, then pass through the security checks, and then fly to CDG airport in Paris and taxi into the city. The train took only an hour more, with a lot less stress. Besides, Alexis was deep in thought about her plan. The first part of the plan was executed while on the train. She noted the time; it was a little after ten in the morning. She opened Robert's email and wrote another reply.

> *My dear Robert,*
>   *You once asked why I didn't just look into my crystal ball if I wanted to see something. I have decided to take your advice. I had my assistant in L.A. FedEx it to me yesterday. I can't wait to peer into its depths every few days. I know that you don't give much credence to my psychic abilities, but you never know. Check your email to see what I see. You may be surprised.*
>   *Alexis*

Of course, there was no answer, but she didn't expect one: not yet anyway. Then, on her laptop, she developed a list of questions that she wanted answered about Robert and his family, underscoring the importance of accuracy and detail, the more intimate the better. Inès and Émile reviewed the questions, shook their collective heads, shifted in their seats, sighed, and groaned, saying something about it being impossible. Alexis reminded them that they were supposed to be the best. And besides, she reasoned, they had a lot more information now than they had when they had begun several weeks ago. Didn't they have a photograph now? She tacitly agreed with them that maybe it wasn't her Robert, but it was certainly a good likeness.

Reluctantly, they seemed to embrace the idea. As their enthusiasm for the chase heightened, they began developing new hypotheses and additional sources for some of the requested information. They reminded each other that the Sorbonne had an archive solely dedicated to the lives of French aristocrats, heraldry, and ancestral lineage. And the Swiss in Bern also housed information pertaining not only to Swiss persons of interest but foreign dignitaries, authors, even a few scoundrels. Which category would the de Valmers fit in?

Nevertheless, Émile felt an obligation to inform Alexis that it would be expensive. There might be more travel, more payoffs, and it would be helpful if they could hire some freelance staffers as research assistants. There were many pages to go through—newspapers, deeds, court records, even church and ecclesiastical records that inscribed birth dates, christenings, marriages, and deaths. Alexis agreed to all of it; at this juncture, she was determined to get her man.

From what she had learned so far, their first knowledge of the de Valmer family was during the mid-eighteenth century, 1750 or thereabouts. In essence, they would be delving into the period from 1750 to 2000; they had about 250 years to account for, since it was no secret where Robert Valmer had been since 1997, when he met his deceased wife, Arianna Soldati.

"It's a lot of years to annotate," Émile noted.

"It is, but if you divide it by fifty, you have approximately five Robert de Valmers to account for," said Alexis. "And we already know the first one and the last one. It's the middle three that we're after."

"But Alexis, even if you know all this, I'm not clear on how this will influence Robert to change his mind about your relationship," Inès said.

"It's not the information itself per se, it's the way I intend to use it."

Inès and Émile nodded assent, but she knew they didn't understand. How could they? She had purposefully left out a very important point—*Henri!* And she was glad she had. She could handle it from here.

A little after ten the next day, lazing in her suite at the George V, Alexis gazed deep into her imaginary crystal ball. While Robert would know she wasn't actually depending on a crystal ball, just a tongue-in-cheek ploy, she planned to keep him busy and guessing. She sent another email.

> *My dear Robert,*
> *My crystal ball is somewhat cloudy this morning, but gradually it is coming into focus. I see an estate somewhere in France. Oh, yes, there it is, it's clearer now. It's the Château de Valmer. And there on the grounds I see a chapel, probably a family place of worship. Could it be that it was the Valmer family chapel? The stained-glass windows, the wooden benches; I see them all. Did a young Robert misbehave on those back benches?*

That seemed like enough for the first installment. He might not be impressed with this first reading, but Alexis was curious to see how he might respond to future sessions. She decided she would not send them every day, and she wouldn't send them in any pattern at all. The next one she would prepare for an overnight arrival. Then she would skip a few days. Her ploy was to tease his curiosity into a state of anticipation about when and if a new message would pop up.

TWENTY-ONE

When Robert left Florence to avoid Alexis, he knew that he couldn't go to Rome as he had intended; that might have been too obvious. How much did she know? He decided to travel to the northern part of Italy to Asolo, a small medieval village north of Venice in the Treviso area at the beginning of the Dolomite foothills. He needed a hideout that was both remote and unexpected; Asolo qualified. It was off the map. He could stay there indefinitely at a luxury hotel owned and operated by the Cipriani family of Harry's Bar fame. He had frequented this little out-of-the-way town many times—times just like these when people began asking too many questions. Asolo was a place to disappear.

At one time, this large Tyrolean house of three floors and an attic had been the home of Robert and Elizabeth Barrett Browning. On this stay, Robert had a corner room looking south across the meadows, where the view was one of a sleepy pastoral green. Robert had just returned to his room after having breakfast on the terrace of the hotel when he decided to check his email. It was a little past ten in the morning. Opening his phone, he saw that a new email from Alexis had arrived only three minutes earlier.

As he read the first sentence, he muttered out loud with some disdain, "Crystal ball indeed."

But when he digested the scope of the email and its stunning accuracy, he became uneasy. Had she actually visited the grounds of the château? Had her detective been there? Had either one of them spoken with that nosy caretaker? Suddenly he wasn't in the mood for a walk; he was in the mood for a drink.

***

Back in Paris, Alexis thought that, for accuracy's sake, as well as integrating herself into the psychic possibilities of connecting with Robert, that she would make the trip to Orléans and the Château de Valmer herself. Inès offered to come along, but Alexis explained that she needed the solitude to meditate and allow her thoughts to ebb and wane with the moment. She urged Inès to expedite the discovery of as many facts regarding the de Valmer history as she could, as quickly as possible. Her strategy with Robert depended on the accuracy of information. In the end, she had to discover on her own the secret he wouldn't reveal.

By noon the next day, she was standing before the Valmer estate's chapel, a landmark site on the historic record of France. She learned from a handout provided at the entrance that the property dated from the early sixteenth century. Alexis toured the inside, but her real focus was the small cemetery somewhere behind the chapel but within the walls of the attached gardens.

Not hurried and yet not wanting to bring attention to herself, she exited by the side door and walked toward the area in the back. When she turned at the corner of the building, she saw the small yet well-tended series of markers and monuments that could only be graves, surrounded by a waist-high stacked-stone wall. These were old memorials, lichen covered and weathered by age and the elements. No recent internments with their new white marble disrupted the serenity or antiquity of the site.

Since no one was around, she passed through an opening in the surrounding wall and began to read the inscriptions on the gravestones. Nearly every name was a de Valmer. There was the Count Guillaume and his son Philippe, who had died within a month of each other, but the most striking of all was the memorial, a large and obviously important one by its size, that was inscribed "Anne Marie de Valmer, beloved wife of Robert and mother of Robert and Hélène." And next to her grave was that of the infant, Hélène, Robert's sister. The baby had died when less than a year old. But most pertinent to Alexis, there was no Robert de Valmer, *père* or *fils*.

As Alexis made her way back to Paris, she wondered how she might use the information she had come upon to the most distinct advantage with Robert. She knew from Émile Hibou's earlier report, when he had visited the site, that one of the caretakers of the de Valmer estate's grounds had seen a man very recently standing for a conspicuously long time in front of the mother's grave. It had to be Robert, and there had to be a reason more important than some interest in ancestry. While she had a few facts regarding Robert Valmer, she didn't have enough to make any definitive judgment. This was therapy without the patient's participation. She was still wondering what could be so horrible that he couldn't tell her. And secondly, how did she fall in love with someone so secretive? Maybe it was the mystery and the challenge. Maybe she just didn't like taking no for an answer. She had always been attracted to the complex if not the impossible.

Arriving back at the hotel, Alexis found a note from Inès. They had been doing some digging and had news for her. Could she meet them the next morning? They would come to the hotel, early if she liked. She called and left a message that they could come at 8:30 for breakfast. This news prompted her to wait to send out the new crystal-ball report until the next day.

When Alexis went down for breakfast the following morning, Émile and Inès were already seated at a table overlooking the garden court of the hotel. They ordered breakfast, then Inès searched through her briefcase and pulled out a ream of papers and began to expand on what they had learned in the past few days.

"Our sources have sent us documents indicating that the de Valmers, Robert and son, fled France in 1793 and showed up later that year in Zurich. We have this record from an old *Grundbuch*, literally meaning 'groundbook,' from Zurich in 1793, which indicates that a Robert Valmer—no longer de Valmer, and at this juncture a naturalized Swiss—purchased a property in the old town overlooking the River Limmat. The house remained in the Valmer name until 1812, when Robert Valmer, the son, sold it to a Swiss attorney.

"There was a notation in the *Grundbuch* when the house passed to Robert the son in his father's estate in 1811. And in the estate documents it is mentioned that the father was buried in Davos, Switzerland. We are still looking for information on the son, who could be the great-great-grandfather of your Robert."

"Great work. But what about the son? Are we at a dead end, or do we have something to go on?"

"After he sold the Zurich house, we don't have any information," Émile said. "We are looking into the Davos records about the existence of a cemetery dating back to the early 1800s, but the Swiss have a way of recycling their grave sites every fifty years or so. It's a small country with limited space."

"Let's not forget the warrant of 1820, the dueling incident," said Inès. "This may be the son who returned to France as a result of Napoleon's defeat and the establishment of the Bourbon dynasty in France."

"But wouldn't he have been too old at that point to be fighting duels?" Alexis asked. "If he and his father fled France in 1793, he must have been at least twenty-five, so add another thirty years and he would have been fifty-five. Do we know what the duel was about?"

"No, not yet," Émile said. "Maybe he was older when they left France. Maybe he married in Switzerland and his son went back to France with him. If he had a son in the mid-1790s, then his son could have been in his twenties when the duel took place. That is more of a dueling age, when young men's egos and pride lead to risky adventures."

"What's next?" Alexis asked.

"We'll continue to follow up on the warrant for the arrest of Robert Valmer for dueling. There must be a record beyond the warrant itself. If we can find any documentation to discover where he went when he escaped, then we can begin to piece together some of the years we're missing. If we can just get into the twentieth century, there will be more records. Unless of course, the Valmers changed their name or used an alias. What will you do? Wait?" Inès asked.

"No, I think I'll go to Zurich and then Davos," Alexis said.

"Do you want me to go with you?" Inès asked.

"No, I think I know what I'm looking for," Alexis said. "And besides, who knows where the trail will go. You may have to go somewhere if a new lead appears. I'll take the sleeper to Zurich this afternoon and then rent a car."

"Inès, I think we have a new detective on the team," Émile said with a slight smile.

Back in her room, Alexis began to pack, but at the same time she was contemplating the next installment of her crystal-ball gazing. She was looking for something in her recent memory of her visit to the Valmer chapel. She searched and searched for something other than the obvious. What had struck her the most when she stood there in the stillness of that mossy glen?

And then it came to her.

Dear Robert, my darling,

Wandering out the side entrance of the chapel at the Château de Valmer near Orléans, a number of gravestones of your ancestors come into view. And one in particular is that of the wife, Anne Marie, of Count Robert de Valmer and the mother of their son, Robert. But my darling, the most poignant aspect is the profile of the mother sculpted on the memorial that bears a striking resemblance to your own profile, considering the shape of the aquiline nose, the strong brow and jaw, and the large eyes. As you once said, the de Valmer genes must be strong. You have a fascinating past.

Love, Alexis

She wondered if this might bring the bear from his cave. She was certain that Robert could fill in a lot of the blanks, so why didn't he?

When she arrived in her compartment on the train, he hadn't responded. That meant they had to play this little game some more. She didn't want to think about the psychological implications of her pursuit of a man who didn't seem to want her. If she didn't know as much as she did about the avoidance syndrome, then she would give up. Robert's case was classic. He was destructive to himself and those he attracted. Closeness and intimacy were emotions to be feared and mistrusted. The answer was always to not let anyone get close, and if and when someone did, he would abandon that person before they could abandon him. Could she convince him that she truly loved him? Would he let her?

***

With the arrival of the third installment of the Alexis history report, Robert knew she was getting help from that French woman, the investigator. He wondered who it was and how Alexis had found such a person who could find these intimate details so quickly. But he couldn't see how anything could ever come of it, and she would soon arrive at a dead end. While he loved her, he couldn't take the risk of revealing the extent of his secret. And her latest observation of there being a strong resemblance between him and a woman she considered to be an ancestor only proved that she wasn't close to the real truth.

TWENTY-TWO

Émile had given Alexis the name of the *Notar* in Zurich. *Notars* are reliable sources of information and the official guardians of the *Grundbuch*, the government document tracing the history of the transfer and ownership of property going back centuries. Not only did it contain the names of the owners of each parcel, but also it contained detailed survey measurements regarding the layout and extent of the property. Every piece of terrain and its improvements had its own unique history meticulously recorded for posterity in those pages.

In the old medieval towns of Europe, where the density of both population and the resulting dwellings was so concentrated, every centimeter was scrupulously guarded. And in many cases, the position of notary is jealously passed from one generation to another. In Europe, the competition for village historian always lies between the parish priest and the notary. Herr Geissenberg, third-generation *Notar*, was the conceded champion in Zurich. The history of property was the history of a town and its families.

Alexis had made an appointment with him at his office, which was in an old building squeezed between two modern glass-and-steel structures in the financial center of town just off the Bahnhofstrasse, halfway between the train station and the Paradeplatz.

On the morning of their meeting, Herr Geissenberg, a very studious-looking and supremely mannered Swiss, invited her into a conference room adjoining his office. Alexis had always been a contrarian of sorts, and today was no exception. Rather than dressing for the appointment in a traditional somber color with a conservative mien, she wore a soft-gray crepe silk suit, a fuchsia-pink scarf encircling her neck. She knew that she was pretty and even prettier when she followed her instinct to flaunt her femininity. Herr Geissenberg made a nervous adjustment to his glasses and then even went so far as to polish the lenses with a handkerchief from his pocket. She could tell he wasn't offended by her departure from the expected business attire, he was charmed. It was a good start.

"Dr. Roth, I'm wondering what further assistance I can be since I have made available to your associates all the information that I have regarding one Robert Valmer," Geissenberg began.

"And we are grateful, and it's been helpful to a point, but we think that Monsieur Valmer came back to Switzerland from France sometime around 1821," said Alexis. "We are trying to discover in which Swiss city he lived upon his return. Did he buy a house in Zurich at that time?"

Geissenberg reflected on her question, looked down at the notes he had prepared for their interview. Then he said, "Well, if that's all you want to know, then there's an easier way to find out. Every person entering Switzerland must have a residence permit if they stay longer than three months."

"And how can I access those records?"

"They're held in the archives of each canton. You would need to know which canton he resided in."

"There are a lot of cantons."

"True, but only a few that would have suited Monsieur Valmer. And I think you can rule out Zurich."

"Why is that?" Alexis asked.

"Because he was French. When he and his father first came to Zurich, sometime around 1793, they couldn't go to Geneva, because at that time it was still part of France. But when Napoleon was defeated,

Geneva became independent and joined the Swiss confederation. Monsieur Valmer was an erudite man, one of sophistication and commerce. The documents directing the transfer of the Zurich property from the senior Valmer's estate to his son indicates a man of substantial wealth, and there were no other survivors mentioned in the testament. I'm certain it was Geneva."

Alexis reflected on the conversation and what she had learned. Most would say that she had learned nothing precise, but there's deduction by addition, and deduction by subtraction. Gradually, possibilities were eroding, leaving fewer and fewer choices. Even dead ends could provide clarity.

Davos was a two-hour drive from Zurich, and Alexis wished that she had hired a driver, as there were beautiful vistas on both sides of the road. She arrived in the late afternoon. She had investigated the town on the Internet, but it was even smaller than she had expected. What could it have been like in the 1790s? Dirt roads or cart paths would have forecast a trip of days from Zurich rather than hours. What had attracted the de Valmers to this tiny valley high up in the Grisons of Switzerland?

The next morning, she didn't ask the concierge of the Intercontinental, where she was staying, about her interest in cemeteries, how macabre, but instead went to the tourist office in the middle of the village. Davos was a two-season resort town that relied on skiing and other snow and ice sports during the winter; in the summer, hiking, golf, tennis, and water sports. During each of these periods, the population more than doubled as tourists from across Europe visited Davos to enjoy its scenery and hospitality.

The predictable but traditional Davos Office of Tourism featured the Swiss affection for pine paneling, cuckoo clocks, large cowbells, and long alpenhorns, which decorated the two-desk, one-counter office. Two rosy-cheeked agents with fair complexions, one female and one male in period costumes, manned the post.

"Guten morgen" rang out in unison as Alexis entered. Of course, they were prepared for her to ask the usual questions about hiking trails and wildflower excursions, but instead she wanted to know

about cemeteries. But more specifically, she asked for information on cemeteries in existence since 1790. But why, they asked quite naturally. She explained that it was about tracing ancestry. They smiled, not able to help much, but when she was leaving, the young man, as cheerily as ever, said, "If you want that kind of information, then you need to ask Herr Glûckmûeller. He's the notary. He knows everything about Davos."

Glûckmûeller's office was literally around the corner in an antique chalet that looked as if it was a part of some of the more official-looking structures of the mayoralty. Two flags flew in front—the Swiss national and the canton flag. Alexis trudged up the steps to the second floor, where a sign in German black lettering announced "Hermann Glûckmûeller, Notar."

Thank God for notaries, Alexis thought. She knocked and interpreted what she assumed was an invitation to enter. A woman greeted her with the universal *"guten morgen"* and asked her if she could help. At least, that was what Alexis hoped she asked. They quickly retreated to English, the default language of the traveler. Alexis indicated her desire to meet the notary and ask a few questions. The woman, probably his secretary, disappeared into the adjoining office, and after a few minutes she returned, announcing that Herr Glûckmûeller would see her now.

Glûckmûeller informed his guests right away through his appearance that he was a formal man. Although at an Alpine resort, he was dressed in a three-piece navy suit, an English pinstripe of classical design. He had thick black hair, every strand in place thanks to a pomade, and black horn-rimmed glasses. His desk and all his papers and pens were lined up in formation. He inquired through a white smile as to how he might be of assistance. Alexis played her best card immediately—her professional business card with PhD degree acronym. He took it in his hand and read it carefully.

Alexis explained that she was researching the ancestry of one of her clients in an attempt to maximize his therapy and the interpretation of his dreams. Further, she asked if there were any really old cemetery plots in the village or nearby.

This question put him in his element, and he was so pleased to expound.

"By custom, cemetery plots in Switzerland do not maintain their integrity for more than a certain time frame, normally fifty years, although there are exceptions. The oldest cemetery, a public one, is Waldfriedhof, but it dates back only to the early 1800s."

"But what about private cemeteries, maybe private chapels or shrines of some kind?" Alexis asked.

"Indeed, and there are two. One of them is on the Zelldorf estate near Klosters, and the other is just outside Davos, connected to a home that is on the national historic register. The home itself sits on a beautiful site overlooking the Landwasser River, which runs through the village. It remains as it has always been for two reasons: one, it is built of stone, and the other is money. It is maintained impeccably, although I have only visited it once, and briefly as a result of official orders from Bern regarding a boundary dispute."

"That's odd, isn't it?" Alexis asked.

"Very odd, but we don't question it. It's just there, and we accept it. They don't allow anyone in, and through a maze of fencing and walls, it is a fortress. Although I don't have any personal knowledge, it is rumored that a sophisticated security system protects the property from even accidental encroachment. There are several caretakers who are carefully selected for their expertise and their rectitude."

"What does that mean?" Alexis asked.

"It means that they don't talk. Funny, too, since all three are Italian. Sicilian, I think."

"You said you visited it once. What did you see?"

"A well-maintained house stocked as if the owners were expected to return from a trip at any minute."

"Who owns the house?" Alexis asked.

"I don't know." He appeared embarrassed that he didn't.

"I thought you were the notary?"

"I am, but somehow the records of this house have been sealed at the highest level," he said, throwing up his hands.

"But what if something happens at the estate, like a fire?" Alexis asked.

"Under that circumstance, we have instructions to call a Zurich bank that holds the trusteeship of the home and arranges its maintenance."

"You indicated there was a cemetery on this property. Did you see it when you visited it that one time?" Alexis asked.

"I did, but it wasn't a cemetery per se; there were just two graves. I suspect one of the graves must have belonged to a previous owner. It was more like a memorial. There was even a huge sculpted sarcophagus."

"Do you happen to remember the name on the tomb?"

"Yes, it was Count Robert de Valmer. I think he was French by origin, although he became Swiss sometime earlier. I think I remember 1811 or maybe 1812 as the year of death on the grave plaque."

"And what was on the other marker?"

"It was blank."

"And what do you make of that?"

"Perhaps at one time it was to be for another person of that family, maybe the wife or a son."

With that news, Alexis thanked Herr Glückmüeller and left his office. She knew that he didn't understand why she was leaving so abruptly. He couldn't know the significance of what she had just learned, because from his perspective, these were all just unconnected facts. She could see by the look on his face that he was wondering how the name on the sarcophagus could trigger such a hasty retreat. Why had she stopped asking questions? He seemed disappointed. He probably didn't receive many visitors, and maybe not too many PhDs.

The next morning, Alexis drove back to Zurich, turned in the rental car, and took the express train to Geneva, checking in once more at the Hotel des Bergues. She couldn't stop thinking about the latest information. She wasn't surprised by the name on the grave, but the fact that a trust had apparently been set up to maintain the house and its grounds since the 1800s as a memorial was of the flabbergasting variety. Robert undoubtedly knew of this arrangement, and more motives were at work than even she could imagine. She didn't plan to share these new revelations with Inès or Émile, and certainly not with Robert. She, too, could have a secret from time to time, and she would wait until the right moment to whisper it in his ear.

TWENTY-THREE

The judicial archives of the cantonal offices of Geneva were in the old town in a series of interconnecting buildings dating from the eighteenth century. Alexis had little to work with outside of a name and a date range. Now she had to depend on the Swiss insistence on accuracy. Still, she was optimistic. If they could construct watches that kept time to the millisecond, perhaps they might have preserved documents that traced the wanderings of one M. Robert de Valmer.

After a few false starts at the information desk, she was directed to the basement, or what the French language designates as the *sous-sol*, literally, underground. It wasn't as bad as that. There were a few windows on one side of the vast room she entered, while the main part of the area was screened off by thick wire mesh. She presented herself to a clerk who was behind a glass partition; he was busy at a computer terminal. She saw that there was a small machine that dispensed tickets that designated one's place in line. She pressed the button, and a ticket rolled out with the number 76 on it. The lighted sign behind the partition read 75. No one else was around. She was next.

She waited about ten minutes. The clerk continued to tap away at the keyboard of the terminal, not looking up or making any other sign that he knew she was waiting. Alexis sat up, adjusting her posture, erect, eyes focused directly ahead, a facial expression of patience and detachment. This man needed to understand that she wasn't leaving. After a few more minutes, he got up from his stool, opened a file drawer, and deposited some folders. Then he turned and announced, "Seventy-six," while advancing the number on the sign. Alexis stood in front of the glass, speaking through the small portal, and asked if the man spoke English. He did. She explained that she was researching the history of a family, the de Valmers, and it was well known that a member of that family had lived in Geneva on several occasions when not residing in either France or Italy.

"Exactly what do you want from the cantonal archives?" he asked. "And let me add that there is a fee for any record retrievals and any photocopying that might be required."

Alexis explained that she understood there would naturally be a cost, and it was not a problem. The clerk introduced himself as Monsieur Blanc and further indicated that a deposit would be necessary. The amount of the deposit would be based on the estimated amount of time that would be expended in the search. And if she still wanted to proceed, then the necessary documentation as to her identity, the reason for the research, and the scope of the search, including as much detail as she could muster, would be necessary as well. She agreed to all the conditions. What choice did she have?

After Monsieur Blanc had provided the form that she was to complete, she sat in one of the chairs and filled out the ten-page form. She approached the window and took another number, number 77. There was still no one else around. Sooner than before, he called out number seventy-seven. He perused her form and indicated a deposit of two hundred dollars in Swiss francs.

"These records that you want from the 1820s are not in this building. They're across the street. And don't you have a narrower range of dates than twenty years? This is going to take a long time. I'm not sure we'll have anything. There's not much to go on except this one name. What about other family members, addresses, birth dates? Anything?"

"I'm sorry. That's all I have," Alexis said.

"I'll have to do it myself. The others are not accustomed to looking for anything that goes back this far. What's this all about? It can't be what you've put down here, ancestry investigation. Normally it's an attorney who's requesting this kind of record. What's going on?"

"OK. It's a wedding present. It's my fiancé's family. It's a surprise."

"I knew it was something like that. Now it makes sense. No need to hide the truth."

"How long?"

"At least a couple of days, maybe more. And give me your telephone number. I'll call you if I have it sooner. *Mon dieu*, this will be a nice surprise for your fiancé."

Two days turned into three, but Alexis was stymied. She didn't want to seem impatient and drop by the archive office or call M. Blanc. The fact that he had said a couple of days and now it was three made her wonder if there was a problem. But she knew from her work as a psychologist that worry is a pastime employed to blunt anxiety. When she returned to her hotel from an afternoon walk along the lakefront, a message from M. Blanc was waiting in her box. It requested that she come to an office on the second floor of the administration building rather than the basement; the hour of ten o'clock was proposed for the following morning. He didn't require a response. It was assumed that she would be available.

M. Blanc waited for her in the ornate lobby of Geneva's cantonal administration building, and they ascended the circular marble steps to the second floor together. As they walked down a long corridor with offices on each side, she noticed that the walls were decorated with Swiss heraldry from each canton of the confederation. They slipped into one of the offices, and on the desk was a sign that announced "M. A. Blanc, Directeur des Archives." She decided to ask: "Perhaps the other day you were in the records room only temporarily? It appears your proper office is here on the second floor."

"Yes, we were both lucky," he said.

"How so?" Alexis asked.

"You were lucky, because if I hadn't been standing in for a few minutes for the clerk, he would have, in all probability, dismissed your request. And I'm lucky, because archives and historical record are my passion, and I love a mystery. Your search combines the two."

"Did you find anything?"

"To my surprise, I found more than I expected, but even when you review all the information, it is quite difficult to understand."

"Why? Are there big gaps?"

"There are, but that's not the confusing part. One or more Robert Valmers lived in Switzerland, either in Geneva proper or in its canton, on several different occasions. What I found were property records, some tax records, and many ingress and egress notations."

"And what makes you think there is more than one Robert Valmer?"

"The span of years. For example, there is a document enclosed in the file that indicates that Monsieur Valmer arrived in Geneva from France sometime in the fall of 1822. As a matter of fact, this person entered several times and exited several times, finally settling in a house in the old part of town on rue Verdaine near the Saint Pierre Cathedral. This house, although probably renovated many times, still stands. And by the way, Monsieur Valmer presented a Swiss passport at the time. I thought you said that he was French?"

"Well, what I meant to say was that the origin of the family lies in France, but it is quite possible that somewhere along the line, the Valmers took Swiss nationality."

"The thing is, it must have occurred before 1821, because he was already Swiss at that time, if you see my point," M. Blanc said.

"Perfectly," Alexis said. She didn't tell him about the Zurich and Davos sojourns. He was confused enough. "Anything else?"

"Yes. He sold this house in 1849 and purchased another home, but on the right bank, very near where the lakeside road and the road that leads to Lausanne currently intersect. It must have been a lovely site for a home; it was probably expensive at the time and astronomical now. Your fiancé's ancestors were well situated, as they say."

"And what happened to that house?"

"It, too, was sold in 1859. And one Monsieur Valmer exited the country from a border point near the Simplon Pass that indicates that he was headed to Italy. That is the last record we have until February of 1944, when I find a new entry stating that an R. Valmer entered Switzerland at a border crossing near Zermatt. This indicates that this person entered from Italy. It is important to note that this is very mountainous terrain and remote, and even more so in 1944. At that time, there were no trains or roads leading to Italy from where this border crossing is located. In addition, the border was heavily fortified and guarded during the Second World War on both sides, so how he made it to the Swiss side is mysterious, and this person would not have been admitted unless they had some form of Swiss identification. The only obvious conclusion is that this person was on foot. A very arduous journey; it suggests an escape."

"But, of course, this couldn't be the same man," Alexis said.

"Of course not, but it could perhaps be a son or a cousin, or just another R. Valmer. There's no way to know."

"Are there any real estate transactions that took place involving anyone with this name after 1944?" Alexis asked.

"This is all I have for now. Unfortunately, the time required for this investigation exceeded my estimate, and I will need to ask you for an additional eighty-five Swiss francs," M. Blanc said.

"That's fine, and thank you, but do you have any ideas about where I might look for more information? I'm trying to re-create a story, and with these gaps, it may not be very interesting," Alexis said.

"I do. Is your fiancé Catholic?"

"He's Catholic but non-practicing."

"But his family is of French origin and undoubtedly Catholic. It appears that the Robert Valmers have spent a lot of time in Italy and were men of substance. As a result, if they were active in any way politically, the Vatican would know about it. I would find a way to look into their archives or have someone else do it."

Alexis took the new information and mentally cataloged it along with the rest of the disconnected shards that punctuated the trajectory of the life and history of Robert Valmer. And M. Blanc had suggested a new idea about how to obtain more information. Alexis couldn't help but have a premonition that this might be a string without an end.

"Dr. Roth," M. Blanc said, almost reading her mind, "don't be disheartened. I'll continue to look and give you a call if I find out anything new."

TWENTY-FOUR

Robert found himself in the unusual position of checking his email more often than was ordinarily his custom, and he was not confused as to the reason. He was wondering when and if Alexis would satisfy his curiosity with a new message. It had been five, no, six days since her last communication. He suspected that the trail she was tracking had gone cold. Reflecting on the entirety of his life, it could be said that he had done a lot, but most of it would not be on record, and he had begun to be more cautious around 1855. And this caution was not taken because he was concerned about anyone learning more about him in the distant future, but rather because he had by chance become involved in Italian politics.

He had, until that point, been living a low-profile life as an investor in Geneva. His specialty had always been in currencies, and from time to time a foray into government-backed bonds if the price was right. And since the time of Napoleon, there had been ample opportunities to finance the adventures of the many duchies and monarchies in Italy vying for territory, treasure, and glory after the Congress of Vienna in 1815, which attempted to reestablish the pre-Napoleonic boundaries in Europe, an undertaking particularly daunting as it pertained to the Italian peninsula, where so many interests and counter interests were unresolvable. Out of the conflict that endured for sixty years arose the desire for Italian unification and independence, termed the *Risorgimento*.

Most of the leaders of this movement were either imprisoned in Italy or exiled at one time or another to either South America or the United States. But one of the more respectable revolutionaries had but to cross the Alps from Turin to Geneva to escape the authorities, where family and friends waited to provide solace and sustenance. Count Cavour was no stranger to the principality of Piedmont, the largest and most important Italian state, and he was an ally of its ruler, Vittorio Emanuele II, king of Sardinia, who would become the first king of a unified Italy in 1861.

Not long after Count Cavour arrived in Geneva, having been expelled from Turin, he appeared and was introduced at the bourse and the various men's clubs. At first Robert was on the periphery of his entourage, but over a few months, Cavour became aware of Robert Valmer's reputation as both a loner and an expert at finance. Unifying a country and raising and supplying an army would take money, lots of it. Of course, bankers make those sorts of loans, but the price of securing such a loan is a function of establishing the risk, which influences the interest rate and the fees that, ultimately, if too onerous, can doom the investment to failure. Better to pay a higher rate of return with a bonus if successful to a person who understands and appreciates risk. That's where Robert came in. Sources informed Cavour that when Valmer latched on to an investment, others were easy to persuade. Robert Valmer was known to not lose any money. People thought that he knew how to pick a horse, though it was reputed he didn't gamble at all.

After the unification was successful and the new national government was established in Rome, Robert left Geneva and settled in Italy for a period of some hundred plus years, except for a short period during the Second World War, when he barely escaped from the Fascists and Germans, arriving in Switzerland after walking the back roads for over five hundred miles. He had traveled mainly at night, hiding by day, foraging off the land and avoiding any contact with people. In the German-controlled Italy of 1944, no one could be trusted.

While Asolo was an enchanting place, it was best appreciated in small doses. Robert was an active man and counted on living a full life replete with interesting activities and people. The hotel was, at its core, either a lovers' getaway or a tourist spot, but in either case any stay beyond a few days could become tedious. Robert was beginning his second week, and he was tiring of paradise. How many vistas, however beautiful, can one consume before indifference takes the place of wonder? And even the meals prepared for the most refined of palates, when appreciated too frequently, soon resulted in a desire to search for more common fare.

Robert was at that point. That's when he decided to go to St. Moritz for a few days, only 150 miles away in Switzerland, about four hours' drive. There wouldn't be a lot more life there than there was in Asolo, but he could play golf and hike and even enjoy some spa treatments. What he really needed was to get away from his thoughts of Alexis. Why couldn't she see that it was best to forget about him? But he wasn't doing such a great job of forgetting her either, so how could he blame her?

Two days later, Robert checked into Badrutt's Palace in St. Moritz. During the winter ski season, Robert always stayed there, the center of social and *après-ski* life in the small village that had been the site of the first Winter Olympics. And in summer it had easy access to several golf courses. The only drawback was that he was more likely to run into people he knew at Badrutt's. He wasn't in the mood to reminisce about old times or to catch up. He preferred to meet new people who didn't have any point of reference regarding his past, a condition that provided him with the opportunity to control the quantity and quality of the information they could know.

He was accommodated in a large suite on the third floor of the grand hotel, one furnished with French antiques and the finest bed linens from Porthault. It was late in the afternoon. Just after dusk, he would be sitting at a window table in the elaborate dining hall overlooking the lake far below, the peaks of the Engadin range outlined in the distance.

But no matter the beauty and tranquility of the location or even the luxuriousness of his accommodations, he was still alone. When he had been with Alexis, he hadn't known where the relationship would ultimately lead, but at times, he had dreamed of traveling with her to the destinations he knew so well. With her sensitivity to beauty, places like St. Moritz and Asolo, not to mention Florence and Rome, would have charmed her. Although she had previously toured some of these spots, he believed he could have provided a whole new perspective and experience they would have cherished together. He grieved that all this was lost. And without a person you love to enjoy a shared story, a certain emptiness creeps into the psyche.

TWENTY-FIVE

When Alexis returned to her hotel after her meeting with M. Blanc, she sat in the bar contemplating what her next move should be. She searched her mind for any connection or person that might have some association with the Vatican. Knowing a lot of people was advantageous, but who did she know that might have a possible in with someone at the Holy See? Even when she went through her address book on her phone, she didn't see any entry that gave her hope.

Deep in thought, she was suddenly aware of a bellman standing directly before her. "Dr. Roth, a package for you."

It was a DHL overnight package; the familiar bright yellow and red Tyvek envelope was handed to her. She saw that it was from Émile Hibou in Paris, and it was thick enough that she struggled to open the flap. Maybe her luck was changing.

A cover letter introduced the contents of the dossier, and after the necessary and formal introduction, Émile got to the point. He explained that Robert had lived in Rome for some time and seemed to be involved in all matters of finance and currency trading. The Vatican, being a major force in Italian, even international, finance, would not have overlooked anyone as talented as Robert Valmer. For this reason, the Hibous had determined to find a contact with ties to the Vatican as well as continuing to follow all the other leads they had turned up. It's as if they had read Alexis's mind.

They were lucky, because Émile and Inès had been corresponding with all their regular sources, including one in Rome who was an investigative reporter for the Vatican newspaper, *L'Osservatore Romano*. Fausto Natali's specialty was business, and it was his beat to report on all facets of the Italian economy and all issues that might impact the Church. As a result of his position—and here Émile intimated that Fausto, while not exactly a puppet of the Vatican, was a reliable voice—he had access to all kinds of databases that pertained to the financial history of the papacy.

To ensure that there were no misunderstandings as to what they were looking for, Émile had sent Inès to Rome to underscore with Signor Natali the importance of their enterprise. The story regarding misdirected inheritances, which Inès and her father had invented as the reason for their interest in Robert Valmer, had intrigued him, Inès reported. But the linchpin of the negotiations centered on an in-consideration payment deposited in a Swiss bank account at Signor Natali's direction. When it was known that the deposit had cleared, Signor Natali—please call him Fausto, he said—was all too eager to help.

In the beginning, Inès gave him only bits of information to test his research prowess and his credibility. Naturally he complained that there seemed to be little to go on—a name, a few dates, and a lot of speculation—but when Inès reminded him that there would be a substantial bonus if her client could be afforded concrete information otherwise unavailable to the public, his enthusiasm for the mission increased. As it turned out, Fausto surprised Inès. He was an old hand at digging around in the archival records of the Vatican, which he jokingly referred to as the catacombs. And he didn't stop there; he also investigated the archives of his own newspaper as well as those of *La Repubblica*, the paper with the largest circulation in Rome, to which he had access. He reported having found the following:

In 1861, an investment company owned by Robert Valmer, Pax International, SA, or PISA, transferred its seat of incorporation from

Geneva to Rome. The transfer itself was a formality, because one of the three fathers of the unification of Italy was Count Cavour, Italian but exiled in Geneva, where he had engaged the considerable talents of Robert Valmer, financier extraordinaire. Every political movement, particularly those that must resort to military force, must have money and lots of it. In general, these wars of liberation, or in this case unification, were financed through long-term bonds with high interest rates. Only speculators with nerves of steel participate in such ventures. This is where Robert Valmer entered and ultimately was rewarded once the unification was complete and Vittorio Emanuele was crowned king of Italy. The Valmer company was allowed this transfer without fee or tax and given a special status as an economic advisor to the new unified Italian state. This royal grant allowed Pax International to place investments and secure funding for the new government that resulted in substantial compensation flowing to PISA. This relationship endured even after Count Cavour's death, as his influence as the first prime minister of the new state had been considerable. From the records, it appears that PISA continued to not only exist but also from time to time to thrive as a result of its participation in Italian government dealings, particularly bonds.

Of course, the most interesting part of the evidence from this particular inquiry was that the primary force and head of this enterprise was none other than Robert Valmer. Moreover, the address for the company, even to this day, was a small palace in the Piazza di Sant'Eustachio near the Pantheon in Rome, though currently the company's affairs were managed by a trust controlled by a Swiss bank in Zurich.

The transfer of management to the bank in Zurich happened in 1939, just prior to the Second World War. This move was fortuitous for R. Valmer, because many companies that had stayed put in Italy had their bank deposits confiscated during the period of 1940–1944. And some records held in the Vatican document how the proprietor of this entity, PISA, had run afoul of the authorities in his suspected financial support of partisan resistance groups opposed to both the Fascists and the Nazis in Italy.

At this juncture in the information, Fausto ventured that the Vatican had preserved these records because while, originally, the Catholic Church had been a supporter of Mussolini, believing that he would promulgate Catholic catechism and interests, it had found over time that Mussolini was only using the power and prestige of the Pope and the Church to further his own aims and ambition.

But as a result of Signor Valmer's suspected partisan sympathies, a warrant was issued for his arrest. However, he was warned of his impending capture, and he went into hiding. It is unclear what happened next, but the rumors were that he had somehow managed to escape to Switzerland; Geneva, it was thought. Then in 1946, after the end of the war, a Robert Valmer returned to Rome, and the entity known as PISA resumed its activities, soon investing in commercial projects in the rebuilding of Rome as well as investments in the 1950s and 1960s in the renewed Italian cinema industry centered in Cinecittà, Cinema City Studios, on the outskirts of Rome, as well as the burgeoning fashion industry.

From that time on, Robert Valmer—he had to be a son of the original—was known as somewhat of a playboy, squiring around young starlets of the American and Italian film community, and apparently independently wealthy, though it was whispered that his money was inherited. This was repeated in a catty way to discount his own accomplishments, as he was considered to be a savvy investor. The currency market was his specialty.

In 1996, there were newspaper reports that a Robert Valmer moved to Florence, where, a short time later, he married a young Florentine model, Arianna Soldati. They soon moved to Rome and into the palace on Piazza di Sant'Eustachio. Unfortunately, Signora Valmer succumbed to cancer in 2013. She was childless. Two years later, Robert Valmer moved to the United States. It was believed that Los Angeles was his destination.

Alexis read the report several times to commit it to memory and assimilate what she already knew with this new information. In a short time, she had filled in a lot of blanks. Unless someone was actually looking around with a purpose, all these details could have been overlooked. Alexis was glad that her investigators were of all stripes and did not have the composite overview of the facts that she had. She had a vested interest in guarding the truth, while the others might not have the same inclination. She did ask herself why she was not more incredulous. Was it because it had been a gradual denouement rather than a surprise discovery? And without more evidence, she couldn't be certain. Only one person could provide her with the definitive truth. She hoped he would come around to it.

At that moment, the telephone in the room rang; perhaps it was Inès or Émile. She answered.

"Dr. Roth, it's André Blanc at Geneva Canton Archives. I shouldn't be calling you, but something has come up that might be of interest. A colleague of mine in the Customs Department called me. He's the one I had consulted previously about the past comings and goings of Monsieur Valmer. It's not supposed to be revealed, but he called me with some extraordinary news."

"And what is that?" Alexis asked.

"A Monsieur Robert Valmer crossed the border into Switzerland from Italy just yesterday afternoon at Puntweil."

"Where is Puntweil?"

"Puntweil is a minor crossing point near the eastern part of Switzerland, near one of our national forests."

"Where would you guess he was coming from and going to?"

"There's no way to tell, but the obvious indications are that Monsieur Valmer must be coming from Venice or somewhere north of Venice. There are many lovely little towns in that area, such as Cortina or Asolo, and he could be headed to either St. Moritz or Zurich."

"I think I need a map," Alexis said.

"By the way, Dr. Roth, I hope you will keep this confidential. I could, along with my colleague, get into a lot of trouble if anyone found out. This is strictly against the rules. Privacy, you know."

"Of course. I will never mention it."

"And one other thing, I've never believed the reason that you gave me about writing a history about your fiancé."

"And why not?" Alexis asked.

"It doesn't matter. I hope you get your man, Dr. Roth. He's driving a dark-blue convertible, a Lancia." He gave her the license plate number.

If she left right away, she could be in Zurich by nightfall and determine if he was at the Baur au Lac, where he apparently stayed often. And if he was not there, the next day she could drive to St. Moritz. There couldn't be more than one or two hotels there where he might stay. But reason gave her pause. If she surprised him, then he would probably bolt like he had before. There had to be a better way, a way whereby he made the decision to come to her. Now how could she arrange that?

It was time to go to Rome.

TWENTY-SIX

Alexis checked into the Hotel de Russie just off the Piazza del Popolo. She took a suite with a proper sitting room that included a desk. She had work to do, and why shouldn't she spoil herself with lovely surroundings? She surveyed the warm shades of ochre and dark green and a deep red that styled the upholstery of the various pieces of furniture and the headboard of her bed. The four large windows, two in the sitting room and two in the bedroom, overlooked the courtyard and garden. She spied the tables, chairs, and umbrellas of the restaurant. The uniformed waiters were just setting up the outdoor seating under the trees that shaded the garden. That would be her luncheon spot when she needed a break from her work. She decided she would reflect on her strategy and begin fresh the next morning.

***

Robert reasoned that by the end of the week, he would leave St. Moritz, and since he was so near Davos, he would stop by the estate and visit his father's grave. He hadn't been to his estate in Davos in many years, although he had attended a one-day conference there more recently, staying in a hotel. The last time he had actually stayed on the property for any period of time was just before he married Arianna. And the only reason he went then was to get away for a week and reflect on his impending marriage. There had been uniform opposition from her family to the union. Arianna's father and her brother had threatened to disown her if she married Robert.

They had made extensive inquiries into his history, like many others before them, and had come up blank. The point he had reflected on was whether he should back out to protect Arianna from being separated from her family. He knew that she wouldn't desert him, but Robert was trying to judge what would be best for her. If she were to be estranged from her parents and her brother, how then could they live in Florence? How could they be happy as a couple if her fate deemed that *she* was unhappy? But his love for her overwhelmed what he knew was the correct path. They married four weeks later; no member of her family attended the ceremony, and after a few bitter months in Florence, they moved to Rome.

While they remained in love for the fifteen years of their marriage, Arianna suffered an unabated sadness that she was unable to set aside, complicated by the fact that they couldn't conceive a child. When Arianna was diagnosed with a cancer of the most virulent type and died just a few months afterward, her brother, Armando, insisted that her unhappiness and depression had contributed to her death, and ultimately, he held Robert responsible for separating his sister from her roots and her family in Florence.

In some respects, Robert couldn't disagree with him. Deep down, he had known even before they were married that it was probably unwise, but he had been selfish and had wanted Arianna for himself. He knew now that he had made a mistake. And he was certain that somewhere in the potpourri of guilt and regret, this chapter of his life was influencing his decision to not put Alexis through something when she didn't know and couldn't understand what she was getting into. He wouldn't be unfair again to someone he loved. He was convinced that there were those who would argue that Arianna had wanted to marry him just as much as he had wanted to marry her. But Arianna was a child compared to Robert's maturity and knowledge of life and its unintended consequences. He told himself again that he had been right to run away from a more serious relationship with Alexis. He didn't want to be responsible for interfering with someone else's life ever again.

His stopover at the Valmer estate in Davos lasted only an afternoon. He had called ahead to the trust in Zurich, and they had advised the caretakers of his visit the next day. The superintendent walked with him around the house and grounds, pointing out what was being done to preserve the property in the manner that had been stipulated by Robert and managed by the trust. He had also telephoned St. Johann Catholic Church in Davos, the main church dating from the mid-1200s, and asked if a priest could come to the estate the next day at noon for a private Mass.

Robert was surprised when Monsignor Hôrschel himself came rather than sending one of his prelates. He had never met the monsignor before. Robert guessed that when the opportunity presented itself for someone to gain entry to the mysterious property, the monsignor decided that he was the right man for the mission.

Robert greeted him at the door, and as they strolled through the garden to the memorial, they briefly discussed the reasons behind the Mass. Robert told him that he might find it unusual, but he shared the same name and was of some undetermined relation to the deceased buried there. Robert indicated he thought it fitting to celebrate a service out of respect for his namesake. The monsignor agreed that it was a very thoughtful and kind gesture. While the priest progressed through the Mass, Robert stood at the end of the sarcophagus, bowed his head, and remembered his father. Robert's memory of him was quite clear. Of course, he was very different from the kind of father one found in today's world. He was a good father for his time: kind, loyal, and honest. The great regret Robert's father had when he died was that he had never been able to return to his beloved France.

At the end of the brief but poignant ceremony, Robert accompanied the monsignor to his car, but before he left, he gave him an envelope and advised that it contained a donation to St. Johann, to be used per the monsignor's preference.

For a few hours afterward, as Robert headed west through the mountains of the Grisons, he was lost in a reverie of things past. As he approached the outskirts of Zurich, his mind began to focus on the present. And with this return to the present, he knew that he needed to decide how his life should move forward rather than dwelling on the past, and that included Alexis. He hadn't heard anything from her for almost a week. He told himself that it was now safe to go back to Rome. He had left Rome because of all the memories there and to start a new life in a completely different environment. Los Angeles had seemed to be ideal until he met Alexis and fell in love with her. Perhaps it was better now to stay in a place that he knew thoroughly and was as much a part of him as France.

Driving from Switzerland down through Italy, Robert took the Autostrada del Sole. He made good time, but it was still a two-day trip unless he was willing to drive for twelve hours straight. Stopping for the night in Bologna rather than Florence, the next afternoon he arrived in Piazza di Sant'Eustachio in Rome, pulling his Lancia into the courtyard behind the ornamental iron gates. He was home.

His housekeeper, Margarita, fetched his luggage from the car. The palace was a piece of classical architecture of three stories. There was a series of rooms on the main floor that Robert had converted to storage and servants' quarters. His apartments were on the second and third floors, including a rooftop terrace that gave a panoramic 360-degree view of the Centro Storico, the historical center of Rome. The walls were thick, the shutters doubled, inside and outside, and the streets narrow and cobblestoned. These conditions maintained a cool temperature inside the palazzo, even in the hot summers. Robert, being a fastidious sort, had renovated the palace several times and redecorated more. The latest version contained a more eclectic contemporary décor with abstract modern art projecting the right mood, rather than Renaissance frescoes and tapestries. All the furniture was of a modern Italian design and manufacture, employing exotic woods, leather, metals, and glass.

And similar to his home in Los Angeles, he had a gourmet kitchen, an impressive library, a grand piano against the windows overlooking the courtyard, a large salon for entertaining, and a master suite on the third floor that looked west toward the Vatican and the Borghese Gardens. It was a palace of his own creation.

Margarita had been his housekeeper for twenty years, and if she had noticed that Robert didn't age very much, she didn't mention it. Robert had solidified her loyalty and her discretion by providing for both her sons' educations, one at the University of Pisa and the other at the University of Bologna. Although it was a large house and would have ordinarily required a staff of domestic help, Margarita had a budget to employ outside assistance for the heavy-lifting projects. But if Robert was going to permanently reside in Rome, this arrangement would need to be reviewed. Margarita wasn't as young as she once was, although her willingness was not a question.

Tomorrow would be the beginning of his new life in Rome. Alexis had probably given up and returned to Los Angeles. It was for the best, he told himself.

TWENTY-SEVEN

Alexis cleared the desk and took the pack of cards from her briefcase. This was her special deck: one that she used rarely and only with the most extreme cases. She didn't believe in tarot or any other paranormal phenomena. But at times she used it because some patients needed reasons beyond traditional psychotherapy. From her perspective it was a visual aid. This deck in particular was an antique edition published by the Mûller Company of Switzerland. The Mûller edition was the most widely used and the most historically accurate of all the tarot decks. In Alexis's edition, a deck of seventy-eight cards, the line etchings, developed centuries ago, were faithfully reproduced, and the images on the cards had been hand painted.

In her experience, the questioner, the person requesting the tarot reading, always admired the exquisite beauty of the cards as an art object as well as their power to seemingly reveal the truth. And the fact that the cards were manifestly antique granted them an aura of legitimacy. Few people could resist the intrigue and their own curiosity, even the mystery of the tantalizing torture of the explanation of card after card laced with the insinuation of the foreknowledge of a person's subconscious musings.

***

Of course, Alexis, known as a clairvoyant and a person able to coach her clients on successful navigation of future events, didn't believe in the telling of the future. She hadn't received a doctorate from Stanford in psychology to revert to inexplicable and capricious theories of divination. But what she had noticed time and again was that patients, or as she called them, clients, all responded to suggestions to the subconscious. The clients themselves were the real tellers of the past, and thus many times, the future. The cards and their posited meanings only provided the patient with suggestible clues that they then rummaged around in their own minds to find and understand. And the skill of the therapist was paramount in these situations. If the therapist didn't have a good understanding of the neuroses of the patient, then it was almost impossible to help him or her release the source of their pathology. And this had been the problem with Robert. Namely, not knowing the specifics of his situation, and obviously he wasn't doing anything to assist the therapist towards greater understanding; if anything, he was an impediment to any resolution.

Was Robert a candidate for a reading? She was betting he was, since now Alexis had obtained the information that Robert had been unwilling to share before. He had all the indications of someone needing to release his emotional connection to the past. For obvious reasons, Robert had always been chintzy with the details, and this stinginess that bordered on clinical paranoia prevented him from realizing his goals, particularly where relationships were concerned. If Robert could be convinced to reveal his secret to just one other person, it might free up his perpetual preoccupation with disclosure. Alexis believed that she was not only that person who could help him but perhaps the *only* person.

But would he participate in the experiment, or would he find it so frightening that he would resort to anger? Or worse, refuse to read her emails? She realized that it wouldn't work to just find him and tell him that she loved him. No, she mustn't find him, he must find her, but only when he was ready. It was her job to get him ready. She opened her computer to her email account.

My dear Robert,

Sorry for the delay, but I had a few things to clear up. I hope you are well, and I miss you.

I realize that you place little confidence in methods that are not rigidly scientific, but my experience informs me that some things that are true are at the same time incredible and not easily explained to anyone. Perhaps you have had an experience such as I describe.

Let's play a little game. I'll tell you your future by considering your past, and you tell me if I'm right. But you must be lenient. I'm not infallible, but maybe I can get close enough that you'll give me the benefit of the doubt.

To play this game, I'm depending on my most reliable deck of tarot cards, and I'll be using just the Great Arcane cards—numbered I–XXI plus the Joker. We shall count on these cards to burrow into the past and sift through the future. After a good shuffle, I've dealt the first ten cards facedown in an arrangement that dates back to Italy and the 1400s. The configuration of the cards is not random or haphazard; a certain position for each card and its alignment with the other nine are indispensable when wanting to achieve an accurate reading.

For example, card two lies on top of card one, and at a right angle to card one. As we proceed through the reading, I will describe where each card is placed in the pattern. As I turn each card over, I will preserve its orientation as dealt. A card that proves to lie in an inverted sense has a different meaning than when it is not inverted or is right-reading.

Normally in a reading, we would begin with you asking a question. Then together we would turn the cards over one by one to answer the question as well as any other issues that would arise. But since you are not present, then I will ask the question for you. It is as follows:

"Where am I going with my life from this point on?"

With the question asked, I'll begin by extracting card number one from its position under card number two. Card number one indicates your current position in life and the atmosphere and conditions under which your life is playing out.

Now I'm turning it over. Oh dear, it's the Hanged Man XII. This card suggests a life in suspension. It intimates an abandonment of one's goals and a reversal of plans. And to get back on track will require strength, determination, and sacrifice.

We'll turn card number two over soon. Don't worry.

Love,

Alexis

***

Robert had just returned from his bank to check on the various transfers he had made from Switzerland. He had forgotten that he had turned his phone off while in conversation with the banker, but now, when he turned it on, he saw the email from Alexis. He read it, and then he read it again. His first thought was that she was playing two games. There was the one game using the tarot cards, which he found more amusing than revealing. And the other was the mind game with which she was baiting him. She didn't need a crystal ball or any tarot cards to prophesize his loss and lack of direction. Hanged man, indeed. He wouldn't answer until she showed him something meaningful. She was clever, though, even if he found it slightly ridiculous. He guessed that was one of the reasons he loved her.

When no message followed the next day, he found himself irritated, and the fact that he was irritated bothered him even more. He guessed this was her intention. She was teasing him, making him anticipate and wait on her next message. She probably used this same trick of suspense-building with her clients. He promised himself he wouldn't fall for this ploy. He would go about his affairs, and if and when a message arrived he would read it in due time.

The next morning, as was his habit when in Rome, he walked to the Piazza del Popolo and had an espresso and a *dolcetto* and read *La Repubblica* and the *NYT International Edition* at his favorite café, Canova. Little did he know that Alexis was less than one hundred meters away at the Hotel de Russie. Before walking back home, he checked his phone, although he had been listening for a buzz alerting him that some communication had arrived. There was nothing. This was ridiculous. He was ridiculous. This game wasn't as much fun as he had thought. *Stop thinking about it,* he told himself for the umpteenth time.

***

Alexis had asked housekeeping to provide her with a large tray, on which she placed the dealt cards in their arrangement. She stored it on a shelf in the closet. This system allowed her to keep the cards in their proper order and made for an efficient transition from hotel guest to fortune-teller.

When she returned from lunch at a small café near the Trevi Fountain, she told herself that it was time for a new session. She retrieved the tray from the closet, put a "Do not disturb" sign on her door, and arranged everything on her desk, including her laptop. She opened up a new message and proceeded to type the results of the next card.

> *Dear Robert,*
>   *I hope you are ready for the second card. This card will identify the current obstacles you confront in achieving your goals and living the fullest life possible. Here goes, I'm turning it over. Now don't freak out, Robert. It's the Death card, number XIII. It doesn't mean that you will die anytime soon, rather it signifies that the past is dead and that there is the possibility of a new beginning.*
>   *Most of the time, death is final, but in this case, I sense that it indicates the end of one thing and the beginning of*

another, or perhaps it pertains to some unfinished business.
It could mean that the moment for transformation has
come. It could foretell the ending of a familiar situation
and the institution of a new era. Life needs to be lived in
the present. No one has the promise of tomorrow.
Love,
Alexis

After typing in his email address, she pressed the Send button. It was around five thirty in the afternoon. She guessed he would be at home, and she imagined that he might just be keeping watch over the phone to catch the next installment.

At least, she hoped he was vigilant.

***

Robert was at home, lounging in the library and reading a book on the latest scientific advances in the field of DNA. He was curious to know if his genetic makeup was responsible for the anomaly of his non-aging. He had tried to think of a way to be tested anonymously and receive the results at arm's length. He didn't think that there would be a marker along his DNA double helix that would reveal the reason for his longevity. But if an indicator turned up, then the researchers could not be counted on to withhold their discovery. Eventually pressure to identify the name of the anonymous donor of the DNA might triumph over privacy. Just as he began to read about the researchers' interest in extinct species, he heard the vibrating sound of his phone humming on the marble tabletop, indicating a message had arrived.

The chances that it was from Alexis were high, since he didn't have contact with many people. Robert grinned as he read the message. He couldn't take it seriously. Death indeed, starting over, the past is dead, unfinished business, how subtle. These generalizations only reinforced his low opinion of any form of fortune-telling, and he also judged that it indicated that Alexis didn't have enough pieces to solve the puzzle. He was impressed but not surprised, however, by her tenacity.

She would give up eventually and go home. And he wished that he knew where she was. He guessed that she wasn't still in Florence, but Armando had said in his note that she was with a French detective, and she had been to Château de Valmer. Maybe she was in Paris. She wouldn't find much in Paris. She wouldn't find much anywhere. Many had tried. Many had failed.

For a moment he thought about answering her. He might still love her, but it didn't change the reality of the situation. He was beginning to think that the only solution was to kill off any love that she had for him. It seemed the only way to arrest what seemed to be becoming an obsession.

TWENTY-EIGHT

There was no answer to her latest email, and she didn't expect one. Robert would not be impressed by fuzzy interpretations. He was a man, and men like to think of themselves as realists. They want to believe that they only accept *prima facie* evidence, upon which they proceed to make rational and calculated decisions. Alexis knew from attending Dodgers games as a child with her father that the best pitch for a batter dug in at the batter's box, one crowding the plate, was an inside fastball, high and tight. Retrieving her silver-tray tarot prop, she sat at the desk pondering just how high and how tight the next pitch should be. She decided on a brushback.

> *Dear Robert,*
>
> *Sorry for the delay in sorting out the next card. There were a few matters to attend to. I had no idea what a lovely town Davos is. I have never been here before, but I'm learning a lot, particularly from the local notary. He's a nice man and has been very informative, particularly regarding private homes and their grounds, one in particular.*
>
> *I am turning the next card, card three. Uh oh, excuse me, someone at the door . . . more later.*

**

Robert had found over the course of the past few days that, in spite of his determination to ignore his phone, he was constantly checking it as if an important contract negotiation were in play. The phone was the first thing he checked when he woke up in the morning and the last checked at night before bed. He vacillated between disappointment and relief when there was no message. And then, when he was walking along Via Condotti after his morning coffee, it came. He didn't wait until he returned home; he leaned against a wall and immediately read Alexis's latest. Only one word jumped off the page: Davos.

Calm down, he told himself. So what if she was in Davos? Because she knows that's where the Valmers ended up so long ago? What would that tell her? What difference did that make? She couldn't get onto the grounds of the estate, even if she knew about it. She couldn't learn much more in Davos, could she? She was at a dead end.

Still, he admired the fact that Alexis and her detective had rooted this out. No one else had.

**

Alexis, meanwhile, thought that a lull of a few hours might tantalize her subject. But she had to be careful; teasing could be close to torture. She had to intimate without accusation, hint but not reveal, and gradually fill in enough blanks to the point that he would know that she might have figured it out. And then someone was at the door of her suite. It was a bellman with an envelope from Inès Hibou in Paris. Normally she called when she had something new.

A few documents, all in French, filled the envelope, but a letter from Inès translated the meaning of the documents and summarized the information and its importance. *How perfect,* Alexis thought, just in time for the continuation of the interrupted email.

I'm back, my darling. And to continue where we left off,
card number three is Junon, the High Priestess, II. This

card represents wisdom and enlightenment, and this card has quite a bit to say.

It informs me that Mademoiselle Daphne de Montclair was married in 1821 to Count Jean Michel de Longchamps at the Cathedral of Dijon in Burgundy. The engagement and subsequent wedding, which had taken place without the normal polite delay, was the subject of gossip not only for its haste but also as a result of the fact that the new Countess Daphne had, as recently as the previous year, been linked to the financier, one M. Claremont, who had been killed in a duel in the Bois de Boulogne. Reports indicated that Countess Daphne was the subject of the fatal argument between M. Claremont and his best friend. The countess gave birth to a son some six months later.

Must be a coincidence, but M. Clermont's first name was "Henri." Can you imagine?

In general, the Junon card indicates greater comprehension of existing facts that often leads to a better understanding.

Love,

Alexis

P. S. I'm off to Geneva.

***

Robert had decided earlier in the evening to turn his phone off. Alexis was smart, and she was no doubt timing her messages for maximum impact. And it was having the desired effect. But he wasn't going to be kept up all night, either waiting on the continuation of the last message or worrying about its contents. He had a light dinner that he prepared of angel-hair pasta with marinara sauce and a mixed salad. And he drank a little more wine than he normally did. Still, he didn't sleep well.

The next morning, determined to ignore his phone, he—with great discipline—left it at home and walked to his breakfast haunt in the Piazza del Popolo. A croissant and two cups of coffee later, the newspapers read for the day, he found that as much as he told himself to walk leisurely back home, before he knew it, he had broken into a trot. *Dammit,* he thought.

He took the steps to the second floor two at a time, grabbed his phone, turned it on, and waited until it booted up. Yes, there it was. The cipher 1 rested beside the envelope icon. He knew it was from her. He read it.

Robert had forgotten about Daphne. He hadn't cared what happened to Daphne. He blamed her and her coquettish ways for creating the tragic confrontation between him and Henri. If not for her, it would never have happened. He would have been able to stay in Paris. His life would have been completely different. He wasn't surprised that she had married a count, and one from the Burgundy region. She wasn't up to the standards of the nobility of Paris or the Loire Valley. Knowing her, she probably had that bumpkin count in Paris before their first child was born. Daphne was aggressive and ambitious and all too clever.

The only thing he couldn't figure out about the email was that his own name was never mentioned. But it was clear that Alexis knew that this was the Henri of his nocturnal mutterings. Why had she omitted any reference or connection? It was so obvious that this was his Henri nightmare, but could she place him as the duelist? He knew she was that smart. And why was she going to Geneva? That had to be the coldest of trails. What else did she know? He began to be uneasy.

TWENTY-NINE

Of course, Alexis wasn't really going to Geneva, but she wanted to make Robert speculate on what she might learn next. And the list of what she knew that he didn't know that she knew was becoming quite long and more detailed by the day. Picking which fact to reveal was akin to a game of chess. She needed to anticipate what impact the new revelation would have vis-à-vis all the other known and unknown facts while contemplating what Robert's reactions might be. She decided to sleep on it, but in the middle of the night, it came to her. She immediately turned the light on and wrote down the whole sequence, not trusting that she would remember it as well the next morning. Although she slept only a few hours after that, she woke refreshed and ready. This new email would take a break from the tarot deck and resort to the more enigmatic crystal ball.

> *Dear Robert,*
>   *Geneva is such a lovely city, situated on the beautiful Lac Léman. You know it well, I'm sure. Today I got up with the thought that I would consult my orb of truth. I've been praying over it for some time, meditating, listening, preparing myself for any teachings it might have. And my patience has paid off. You probably could tell me what it all*

*means, if you only would. I have seen and listened to hear
what is distinct yet at the same time unclear. The letters
P, I, S, A. Could it be the town Pisa, Italy? Or is it an
acronym of some kind?*

*And quite apart, but linked in a confusing way, I see
high finance. I see war. I see Italy. I see an older man with
a beard and round spectacles, an Italian, a man of the 19th
century. He has a name that I can't make out, but it seems
to begin with the letter C.*

*I'm so tired from concentrating. I need to stop now,
but I'll take another look soon.*

Love,

Alexis

***

After reading her next message, Robert knew that Alexis had learned
about PISA and the Cavour connection during the Italian unification
movement. *So what?* he assured himself. She might guess that the
Robert Valmer in all these time frames was one and the same. But
without any proof—and there was none—then how could her
conjecture become certitude? But a more immediate problem was
that it wouldn't take her long to discover that PISA had an address in
Rome—and that it was Robert's residence as well. Would she soon be
knocking at his door? Maybe the best thing would be to see her, but it
was a risky move since he was still in love with her. He worried that if
they were together again, they might gloss over the problems and, as
optimistic lovers, ignore reality.

No matter what, Robert concluded that he wasn't going to run
from her again. But he wouldn't make the first step. He wouldn't
respond no matter what her tarot cards, her crystal ball, and her French
detective turned up. From his perspective, she would either run out of
loose ends to tie up or the patience to pursue a recalcitrant quarry. He
instructed Margarita to keep the iron gates leading to the courtyard

and the front door of the palace locked. And if by chance someone dropped by, then explain that Signor Valmer was out of town.

***

Alexis was confident that Robert wouldn't respond to her emails until she confronted him with her knowledge of his secret. Knowing his personality and the nature of what he was avoiding, he was counting on the certainty that no concrete evidence existed that could prove the point. From his perspective, she could only speculate what it all meant. His reasoning would predict that she would think that there was a line of Robert Valmers spanning several hundred years, and that the Valmers were a prominent and wealthy family involved in finance, politics, and the social and cultural climate of each cycle. What could be more ordinary or expected? Why look for some meaning beyond the apparent and the reasonable?

Alexis waited several days, both to tell herself that she was being patient and to reflect on the next move in her chess match with Robert. She thought about all kinds of scenarios to pursue but dismissed most of them as too cute. Learning the address of PISA, Robert's company, was as simple as asking the concierge at the hotel. And it was all she could do to restrain herself from marching over to his residence near the Pantheon—it was less than a quarter mile from her hotel. But what would she say even if he answered the door? Another option was to wait outside his home until the blue Lancia came through the gate. Or maybe he would walk to a nearby café in the morning for a coffee, as was his habit in L.A. She couldn't do either, refusing to think of herself as a stalker.

It was time to put all the cards, the tarot included, on the table. The concierge of the hotel engaged a limousine and driver to take Alexis to the Campo Verano. She brought her laptop along. Situated in the eastern part of Rome near the university, Campo Verano was Rome's most storied cemetery, established in the early 1800s. It was the final resting place for most of Rome's VIPs, past and present.

Contrary to what she expected, there were no crowds. She didn't see a soul around as she found the records office in the administration building. Everything was marble—the buildings, the headstones—and it was as quiet as a tomb. But inside, behind a marble reception counter, an older woman dressed in black rose from her chair as Alexis approached. She asked if she could help, in English.

"Thank you. I'm here in Rome for a short time, and I'm a friend of the Valmer family. I would like to visit the grave of Signora Arianna Soldati Valmer."

She didn't need to look it up, but said, "Her resting place is in the Catholic section, a five-minute walk," giving her a map, which she marked.

"How will I recognize it?" Alexis asked.

"You'll have no trouble. It's quite impressive, and you will see the fresh bouquet of flowers that are delivered daily and placed on the tomb."

Alexis went back to the car and informed the driver that she might be an hour or more. He said he would wait, and he offered to accompany her. She countered that she needed the time alone to meditate. He said that he understood.

Twenty minutes later—she got turned around for a few minutes—she arrived at Arianna's grave. Actually, it was more like a memorial. A low wall constructed of slabs of travertine marble about a foot high with a low hedge of dark-green boxwood enclosed the ten-meter-square space. At each corner of the square, an Italian cypress tree, very common in the hills of Tuscany, had been planted. Then in the center on a pedestal stood the Christian cross, majestic in a white alabaster marble; it faced east to catch the rising sun. And at the base of the cross rested a large urn with white calla lilies. The marker read:

Arianna Soldati Valmer

5 Maggio, 1970–20 Novembre, 2013

L'amor che move il sole e l'altre stelle. Dante

***

Cemeteries are thought provoking. The quietude and serenity offer a mourner or a visitor an environment in which to reflect and meditate. Questions arise about the meaning of life, the inevitability of death, and if the life one is living is at its fullest.

Alexis sat on a bench directly across the gravel path from Arianna's grave and concentrated on the scene, much as an art historian might consider a master painting. The symmetry and the symbolism of the monument, including the square shape, the cypress spires, the pure white cross, the lilies, all spoke of Robert's devotion and love as well as his taste and knowledge of classicism. She could also understand how difficult it must have been for Robert, so blessed with such a special gift, to lose his wife at such an early age. Alexis was certain that he would have rued the irony of the situation. At the same time, she began to comprehend his resistance to fall in love again. What might make him change his mind?

She took out her laptop and wrote him another email, this one much shorter than all the others.

> *My dear Robert,*
> *It is love that moves the sun and the other stars.*
> *Love,*
> *Alexis*

THIRTY

Robert felt the vibration of the arriving message, but he wasn't going to ruin his lunch. Alexis's emails had been somewhat amusing at first. That was before, when he felt safe from her probes. He had been anonymous, or tried to be, all his life. She wasn't close to the truth, she couldn't be, but her persistence was disturbing. What if some clue was out there of which he was unaware?

He needed someplace quiet to read the email, away from his home and away from people. He walked toward the Piazza Navona and up the steps into the church of Sant'Agnese. Only an older couple stood in front at the altar. Robert found a place in one of the rows of wicker-backed chairs halfway down the left aisle. Robert didn't attend Mass, nor did he believe in God, but he did find churches reassuring and peaceful. It made him think that perhaps there was something greater than himself.

He opened the message, and the quotation from Dante, the one he had purposely researched for Arianna's eulogy, swept across his memory like a squall sweeps over a boat. Snapshots of that late morning paraded across his psyche, and he felt the sadness he had felt that day with the same intensity. At first, he thought it cruel that Alexis would remind him of this painful period. But then he wanted to believe that the inscription regarding love and its power was her real interest. She had to know that he was behind the setting as well as the tribute.

The other obvious reality was that Alexis was in Rome. And he would imagine her being either at the Hassler hotel or the Hotel de Russie, both in walking distance from his home. She was exhibiting what he knew to be true about her. She was determined, strategic, with a will of iron. God, she was magnificent.

At least she hadn't couched this communication in any mumbo jumbo of tarot or psychic phenomena. Maybe she was beginning to see why he had not been ready for a new relationship of any permanent nature. Perhaps she would even come to the conclusion that his reluctance was based on the tragedy of his wife's death and that there was no other secret to discover. If this turned out to be the case, it would be best for all concerned. He wished it were different, but it couldn't be. He left the church, not feeling worse but better. He felt that they were, or perhaps more precisely, she was, coming to the end. Soon it would be over.

***

Alexis had taken a risk sending an email referencing Robert's late wife, and she hoped that of the several ways in which to interpret her message, he would land on the one that she had intended. Of course, she couldn't know that he had done just that.

Now he would realize that she was in Rome and could probably find out which hotel she was in, or he could guess. She had no illusions that he would call or pass by. The coup de grâce was coming, just not yet.

The next morning, Alexis checked out of the hotel and flew to Paris. She had sent an email to Émile and Inès, asking them if they could meet her at the George V the next morning around ten. They responded in the affirmative without inquiring about the reason for the meeting. She loved both of them. They were so correct, so discreet, and so French.

At ten, the front desk called her room and informed her that M. and Mlle. Hibou were in the lobby. Alexis asked that they be accompanied to her suite. When they arrived, they both gave her a more affectionate embrace than the more or less perfunctory air kiss. They seemed glad to see her again, and she admired how they waited, not showing any impatience or haste.

She asked them to sit down in the sitting area of the suite, and she opened by saying, "It's over."

"Did he call you?" Inès asked, taking Alexis's hand in hers.

"No, I never heard from him." She looked away, embarrassed by her defeat.

"It's a pity," Inès said.

"I know, but it's time to stop," Alexis said, recovering somewhat.

"Papa, you're very quiet," Inès said to her father.

"I'm quiet because something is not right about this," Émile said, getting up and beginning to pace. He was muttering to himself.

"I couldn't agree with you more. But he doesn't want to be found. I must give up. I'm returning to Los Angeles," Alexis said with some finality.

The Hibous commiserated with her regarding how shortsighted and foolish Robert was. They expressed regret that she had spent a lot of time, money, and emotion and now was going home empty-handed. They probably guessed that Alexis Marans Roth hadn't known defeat much in her life. She reassured them by being remarkably buoyant under the circumstances. Alexis indicated that her decision had evolved over several weeks, and by now it was becoming palatable.

***

It was the third day since he had received the last communication, and he had predicted that another one would follow without delay. But Alexis had wrong-footed him again. He had become accustomed to her attention no matter its implications. Any attention was preferable to none at all. He reassured himself that it would be better if she just gave up. He even said to himself that he would be better off if it occurred sooner rather than later. Three days became five. He called the Hassler. No, there was no one by that name at the hotel. He tried the Russie. Yes, Dr. Roth had been there, but had checked out a few days ago. And no, there was no information as to her destination.

THIRTY-ONE

Alexis returned to Los Angeles. She had spoken with her parents just a couple of times while she had been in Europe. They, particularly her father, always wanted to know more than she was prepared to tell them, but she went over to their house the next day after checking in with her office, knowing that she might as well get it over with.

After giving them the highlights of what she had been doing, while not revealing any pertinent information, she admitted that she hadn't been able to find Robert. And she confessed how disappointed she was that he had never responded to any of her emails save one, and that hadn't amounted to anything. Martin was incensed. He regretted over and over that he had ever made the introduction, and he cursed the expense of looking for this cad without any return on the investment, even if it wasn't his money.

Her mother, always the more insightful of the two, asked, "But, my darling, are you still in love with him?"

"He's made it very difficult," Alexis answered.

There was nothing more to say. She pleaded exhaustion and promised that she would come to dinner after she had recovered from the ordeal and the jet lag. They mentioned they could plan something next week, but she postponed. As an excuse, she reminded them that she had a practice to rehabilitate, although her clients had resigned themselves to telephone therapy while she had been away.

Besides, she thought, *I have one more email to send.* It had been long enough between communications; enough time to build anticipation of what was yet to come. *Let's see how he handles this one,* she said to herself.

> *My dearest Robert,*
>
> *Before I left Rome, I took a tour of Cinecittà. I hadn't realized what a history Italian cinema had and how far back it went. My interest was piqued because, in my research regarding Robert Valmer, I came across the fact that your company, Pax International, had invested in several movies prior to your marriage to Arianna Soldati. And my darling, as you are aware, the paparazzi love film starlets and love to take photographs, particularly candid ones when the persons photographed are unaware.*
>
> *Mina dei Fiori, a beautiful Italian star, is sitting in a café in St. Germain in Paris. And with her is a most attractive and debonair man. Why, I would recognize him anywhere, because he looks just like he did when I met him in L.A. a short time ago. But Robert, the funny part is that the photo I'm looking at was taken in 1995. And I know that this is true because a newspaper in the photo has that date.*
>
> *Exhausting all reasonable explanations, it took me a long time to come to the only conclusion possible. And without the knowledge gained in these past few months, I would not have been able to put it all together. It's too incredible.*
>
> *Just to let you know, I could have been trusted with your secret if you had been willing to share it. I loved you that much, but don't worry, my darling, it's safe with me.*
>
> *Love,*
> *Alexis*

When she finished, she looked at her watch. It was eight thirty in the evening. Perfect. It was five thirty in the morning in Rome. He would have some reading material with his coffee.

Although she was tired from the trip and all the expended emotion, she didn't sleep much. She had a turbulent night, wondering if she had done the right thing in letting Robert know that she knew. At this point, she couldn't explain what her goal was.

But there was only one person who could help her organize her thoughts.

***

Robert had never considered how he would feel if someone else learned of his incredible situation. When he began reading the latest message, which he did the moment he got up, he presumed within the first few lines that Alexis had found more history regarding Robert Valmer. Even the mention of Cinecittà and Mina dei Fiori was not alarming, but then the mention of a photo, St. Germain, Paris, and then the telltale date of the newspaper linking his current appearance as being the same as that of a particular date twenty years earlier; he was certain—she knew. He repeated it to himself several times before he read the last lines about her love and that she would keep his secret. She said that now, but over the longer term, wouldn't it come out? Perhaps even inadvertently? Not everything is done maliciously, he reasoned.

What would be the best thing to do now? he pondered. *Should I respond? Should I remain distant and resolute?* Her offer of secrecy was generous and caring. Didn't it demand some kind of recognition, some kind of thanks? He couldn't make up his mind, so he did nothing but wait, but he didn't have much hope of any additional messages from Alexis without some move on his part. There was no one to ask. And what was left to say anyway?

***

Alexis called Aaron Mendelssohn the next day and left a message. He was in session with a patient. It was about forty minutes before he called her back. She looked at the clock; it was five before the hour. He was between patients.

"I need to talk to you," she said.

"It's that bad? How about three?"

"See you then."

Alexis knew that Dr. M—as Robert had called him—was being placed in a difficult position. He was being asked to help, but he wouldn't have all the facts. She couldn't go back on her promise to Robert just to have some peace for herself. She was counting on Dr. M's uncanny insight to give her some perspective on the Robert matter.

At the start, they were more formal than was their habit. Dr. M was as serious as she was and didn't bring any of his usual levity into the conversation. He didn't ask any questions. He listened. He was waiting on her and offered her one of the chairs in front of his desk rather than the couch. It was rare for a psychologist to meet with another psychiatrist regarding a personal matter, particularly if friends, so Dr. M must have decided that they would discuss whatever she had on her mind as equals rather than as doctor and patient.

"Since the last time I saw you, I've been in Europe. And while I found out a lot about Robert, I never found him," Alexis said.

"But you came home," he said. "What does that mean?" He leaned forward as if to better hear her answer.

"It means that I gave up." Alexis frowned, hating that her mentor would see her defeat.

"Was it time to give up?"

"I don't know, but I did."

"You must have had a good reason," he said, his voice full of empathy and understanding.

"I did. I wasn't getting anywhere. I knew the problem, but I couldn't do it all alone."

"Did you fall in love with your patient?"

"But he wasn't my patient," she said, her defenses rising. "He was yours."

"Only by proxy, my dear."

"That's why I love you."

"Do you still love him?"

"Yes." She looked down in resignation that this was the principal problem for her. She loved a man who didn't love her. Or so it seemed.

Her session, even with the stiff preamble, only lasted twenty-five minutes. Dr. M, since the very beginning when he was her professor and counselor some twenty years before, remained the wisest man she had ever met, never excited, always sane. She pitied those without this kind of friend.

She had never even considered that somehow Robert had begun as a lover, and in her perfectionism, she had allowed herself to become his unsolicited therapist. Her father had been right all along. The moment she put on her therapist hat, she began treating Robert differently. It echoed what her father had said: "Did it ever occur to you, Alexis, that maybe you're too nosy."

It was all clear now. It wasn't his secret that had caused the separation; it was her meddling. She couldn't just allow herself to enjoy the present; she had to know his past—all of it. She had been too clever. When they had been together, she had been interviewing him, if not interrogating him. She had been competitive with his intelligence and savoir faire. It dawned on her that she had been showing off. The realization that she had been even semi-responsible for rupturing her opportunity at happiness with him was depressing. Why had she been so foolish? Why hadn't she seen it, when it was so obvious to Dr. M?

The next day, her guilt was no less. She had a difficult time concentrating and found that her thoughts were wandering afield even when she was talking to clients. They didn't notice, but she did. She vacillated from remorse to regret. Should she apologize? Should she come clean? Would it make any difference? It had been months since they had seen each other. Would it matter that they remained in each other's thoughts?

THIRTY-TWO

Dr. Mendelssohn was making detailed notes regarding his last patient's admission that she had been having suicidal thoughts as a result of her husband's infidelity. He had tried to persuade her that abusing herself was no way to punish him. And it was futile to punish him because whatever means she tried to use would only end up harming her. He had also called in a prescription for twice-daily doses of Valium for her until he could help her adjust to the reality of the situation. His telephone rang; it was his receptionist. She said, "Dr. Mendelssohn, Robert Valmer is on the line." She put him through.

"Dr. Mendelssohn, it's Robert Valmer."

"It's been a long time. Where are you?"

"I'm here at my house on Rodeo. I need to see you. Today, if possible."

"How about four this afternoon?"

"Fine, I'll be there. Please don't tell Alexis."

***

Robert wasn't sure if his last request was unnecessary or insulting. Dr. M wouldn't call Alexis without knowing more about why he wanted to see him, and maybe not even then. He might need to apologize later to the good doctor.

His decision to return to L.A. had filled him with doubt. He wondered whether it was prudent, and he questioned how possible it was to resurrect what he and Alexis had had. He fantasized about picking up the pieces of their relationship and moving forward. Many couples did it with some success. No relationship was perfect. And while they had baggage, he understood he had more than most. Was it possible for them to live in the present and not constantly rehash the past? He wasn't sure why he had called Dr. M rather than Alexis. Perhaps he was afraid that she would reject him either out of anger or revenge, given how he had treated her. Maybe Dr. M would have some ideas about how to approach her. They were both sensitive to psychological issues. Dr. M would know her state of mind. Yes, he was certain that Dr. M was the best way to contact Alexis. Robert wondered if she, too, had visited him since she had returned. It had been two weeks since the last email.

Robert arrived a little before four and waited only a couple of minutes before he was shown into the office. After a hearty handshake, he took his usual place. Dr. M wasn't going to help by paving the way. He was waiting for Robert to state the reason for his unanticipated visit. Robert had been relieved when the doctor had agreed to see him the same afternoon. He could very well have proposed sometime next week. It was definitely his turn.

Robert stood up. "Do you think it would be completely crazy for me to call Alexis?"

"What would you say to her?"

"I would tell her that I'm sorry." He sat down again in a heap.

"What are you sorry about?"

"Sorry I left so abruptly. Sorry I didn't respond to her. I'm sorry how it all turned out." He said all this in a hushed tone. He was ashamed that he had been so heartless, but at the time he'd thought he had a good reason.

"Maybe she's sorry, too."

"Why should she be sorry? She didn't do anything."

"She might disagree with you." This statement offered a ray of hope.

"How?" Robert said with some enthusiasm.

"Let her tell you."

The conversation wasn't proceeding at all as he had anticipated. Dr. M hadn't told him anything but had also told him a lot. He hadn't said anything Robert understood, but he knew that what he thought he understood was probably wrong.

"Do you think we could make a go of it long term?"

"Does anybody know whether they can make it long term? It's more how you work on it every day, the short term."

Robert now knew how Plato's students must have felt. Every question was answered with a question. It seemed Dr. M's therapy was based on some mixture of Greek philosophy and Buddhism, a kind of inscrutable truth.

"I kept a secret from her," he confessed with a deep sigh.

"Did you have a good reason?" Dr. M clasped his hands in front of himself, waiting for Robert's answer.

"I thought so."

"Do you still think so?"

"It doesn't matter, because she found it out." He slumped, hoping he wouldn't ask what she found out.

"Was she angry when she found out?"

"She didn't seem angry." Dr. M showed little expression, and Robert wondered if he might know more than he revealed.

"Then maybe she agreed that you had a good reason."

Robert so wanted to ask if Dr. M had seen Alexis, but he knew that he shouldn't. No use in insulting him again. Twice in one day might be too much. Maybe he would hint.

"Should I call her?"

"I'm not sure that you can't call her."

"Me either."

"Do you love her?"

"Yes."

"I think you have the answer."

"Could you give her this?" Robert said, handing him a small envelope.

"Why don't you give it to her yourself or send it to her?" He didn't look at the envelope.

"It wouldn't be the same. Just this favor. It means a lot."

"Do you want me to tell her that you're here?" Now he placed the envelope on the side table, which Robert took as a good sign.

"Yes, but only after she has the envelope."

***

Dr. M didn't want to alarm Alexis, so he called her the next morning and said that he had been thinking about their conversation and perhaps they should discuss it further. Of course, her preoccupation with Robert was all she thought about anyway, and she didn't have a better person to talk to. They agreed on eleven.

Once in his office, she didn't wait to see what he wanted but rather began telling him how Robert had become an obsession and that she was filled with blame and shame as to her culpability in the failure of the relationship.

He interrupted her, saying, "Robert asked me to give you this." He handed her the envelope.

She looked stunned. "Have you seen him? Did he give this to you in person?"

"I think you should open it."

Alexis opened the envelope and took out a card. The card was blank except for what was taped to it. She looked at it. She turned the card over and looked on the back. She looked in the envelope to see if there was anything else. She gave the card and the envelope to Dr. M. He looked at it, too, but without any expression of surprise or puzzlement.

"What does it mean?" Dr. M. asked as he gave the envelope and card back to her. Alexis sat silent. There was a meaning, but what was it?

"Robert said that there was a secret, but you found out. Maybe it's something about that."

"Maybe so."

"A lock of gray hair. Strange," Dr. M said.

She had it. She finally understood.

"When did you see him?"

"Yesterday."

She kissed Dr. M on both cheeks and ran for her car in the garage. In ten minutes, she was in front of Robert's house on Rodeo. She got out of the car, ran to the front door, and rang the bell. He must have expected her, as he opened the door immediately. They both simply stood in the doorway, not quite sure of what to say or who should go first. They eyed each other, taking in every expression, any body language, or the slightest change. It was then that she noticed that he now had a hint of the most distinguished salt-and-pepper hair.

Then Alexis took the lead, holding in her hand the card that he had sent her, and said, "Does this mean that we will grow old together?"

He smiled and said, "Now which tarot card told you that?"

ABOUT THE AUTHOR

Gary Dickson is an inveterate traveler and a Francophile *sans merci*. Educated in the United States and Switzerland in history, literature, and the classics, Gary lives in Los Angeles with his wife, Susie. Gary is also the author of *An Improbable Pairing*, *A Spy with Scruples*, and *The Poetry of Good Eats*.

CPSIA information can be obtained
at www.ICGtesting.com
Printed in the USA
FSHW020135160620
71213FS